Platinum Quest

Dr. Thomas Bagot

Platinum Quest
Third Edition October 2014
Print ISBN-13: 978-0-9873646-0-9
Print ISBN-10:0-9873646-0-X
Platinum Quest (Electronic)
E-Book ISBN-13: 978-0-9873646-2-3
E-Book ISBN-10: 0-9873646-2-6

DEDICATION

Andrew, Jo, Judy, Natalie, and Wendy, without
whose help this book would not have been possible.

Dr. Thomas Bagot

First Published by

BACLESIT

November 2012

Dr. Thomas Bagot

An Important Development has been Sabotaged
A Family's Future is to be Destroyed
A Pristine Environment will be Trashed
Lower Economic Standards are being Fostered

Platinum Quest Synopsis

A rich platinum deposit is being carefully developed by Ben de Bruin, his family, and a small tribe. The development is designed around a consideration for the people and for the ecology of an African wilderness. It is hamstrung by unexplained failures, incorrect technical advice, and underfunding. These difficulties are compounded by a failure of high technology and critical equipment.

The partners are dragged toward physical and financial disaster. Great danger stalks. If Clare de Bruin can be stopped, in any way, from meeting with prospective financiers, Jack Anders, the temporary head of a corporate empire, GVN, will have won. A polished executive, Jack works, in the shadows, toward power and fortune. His efforts include a drive to defraud the heir to the GVN corporation.

An influential consultant, Matthew Clement, and an associate, Rebecca Rosslynn, might be able to help Michael Anders, the heir to the GVN corporation, and Jack's other intended victims, the family, and the tribe. They, too, become a threat to Jack's maneuverings.

The story moves forward, through the Botswanan bush, Vancouver, and South Africa. The character's efforts, faced with several twists, lead to a challenging conclusion.

Dr. Thomas Bagot

1

Clare de Bruin strode briskly toward Stanley Park, from the luxurious Westin Hotel, on Vancouver's Bayshore Drive.

She shivered, cold and afraid. Her fear came from the knowledge that her efforts to find finance, to back the de Bruin family's ongoing development work on a new mine, would block Jack Anders, and that her failure would take him close to his goal of taking personal control of the new mine.

The family knew that Jack had already killed to achieve his ambitions.

A mishap, that took her off the scene, would take him to his long term objective, bankruptcy of the Ngami Platinum partners, and control, not only of the new mine, but of the entire fortune that the Ngami platinum project represented.

Her fears were well founded.

She was being followed by a man who had been told to kill her. He was far more desperate than Clare. Someone who, like the de Bruins, had been driven to his limit by the global crisis and the pressures arising from it.

From a solid Northern English trades background, he had failed in the eyes of those who mattered to him, by being retrenched. This had led a series of bad calls on his part, and his current desperate need for money.

He had been told to kill Clare, because the slick corporate efforts of Jack Anders and van Zyl, to sideline her, had failed.

The cold was intense but the sky was clear. Early morning sunlight caused a high mist to glow. Multitudes of native and exotic botanical treasures grew beneath the tall cedars crowning the huge park. The effect was almost ghostly, threatening. The cold, the environment, and her fear, tempted her to put off her planned walk, but she was frustrated and needed the exercise to recover from a stress filled morning, so she strode on toward Stanley Park.

The de Bruins and the Ngami tribe's efforts in pristine tropical, Ngami, Botswana, were being carried out to high standards of care; for all their employees, associates, the mine, and the African countryside.

Jack Anders planned, not only to steal the resource, but to reduce the cost of it's operation, by using careless and cheaper mining methods.

Clare's being in Vancouver was an extension of efforts she had been making to find finance for Ngami in London.

Just hours before the walk in Stanley Park, she had been striding toward a date, along South Audley Street, in Mayfair, looking forward to having breakfast with an exciting new friend.

Not far from Grosvenor Square, she was stopped by an expected message from Ben, her brother, who she had advised of another failure to secure the project's needed extra finance, the previous day, one they had thought had presented a good chance of success.

Standing next to one of Mayfair's beautiful old stone houses, she read and reread what he wanted her to do, feeling like refusing outright.

Ben wanted her to drop her London efforts to find finance, and leave immediately for Vancouver, to meet with Rebecca Rosslynn about helping get the backing the family needed to keep going.

She stood for a moment, staring into the distance, utterly frustrated, then turned and walked, slowly, along South Audley and into Mount Street, toward a shop on the corner, trying to gather her wits. She stood, gazing, into the window display, at first unseeingly; then, realizing that it was Purdy's, Ben's favorite spot for window shopping, during a previous trip to London, said out loud, "Oh damn, Ben."

Her plans for breakfast, in the gentle dignity of the quaint tearoom, were fading.

A passerby slowed to admire the tall, somewhat angular, athletic looking woman, with cornflower blue eyes, blond hair, and eyebrows a darker shade of blond. Her tailored, fine wool, light gray suit, worn under a darker gray overcoat was complimented by a rust-colored scarf, and a blouse that was a shade or two lighter. She had high cheekbones and slightly slanted eyes. He was reminded of someone he once knew from a Slavic country.

However defined, Clare was attractive and well proportioned. Her shoes, more than her clothes, were a reflection of her personality—elegant, yet well suited to walking.

Not so clearly visible was that she was lonely. The intense work she had undertaken, as the financial expert in the family company, had taken up much of her life.

"I might as well be in a desert, as in one of the best parts of London," she thought, then catching her image in the shop's window, added out loud, "So elegant and so lost." She sighed, she knew how much Ben had achieved. But, she thought sadly, Ben did not understand her feelings.

She used the phone to compose her reply. "The new Ngami mine's share price is drifting lower. We don't have time. Going to Vancouver will delay the financial restructuring I'm arranging. The price of the shares is very volatile. We must act now in case the price drops so far that their value won't provide enough equity for what we need to borrow."

Ben replied immediately, "You told me that every one of the people, to whom you've spoken, needed a certified reference, from a recognized authority, as to the project's capability. I can't get you one."

"How will going to Vancouver help?" she messaged.

"Rebecca Rosslynn is well connected in North America and knows the project's worth. She might be able to carry our search, for finance, over the line. Try to delay the exploratory meetings in London, that you still have planned."

She glanced at the array of quality shotguns and related accouterments in Purdy's window, she thought of Ben's love of the outdoors, and his straightforward nature. She knew that she could trust his opinion.

"Where do I meet her?" she messaged.

"There's a conference at the Westin Bayshore. I'll email Rebecca to say you're going to be there."

She agreed.

Ben concluded the exchange with the warning, "Leave without anyone knowing where you're going. We only have a few days before the bank forecloses."

"Jack Anders can't be controlling the bank though, surely?" she replied.

"I'm getting too much pressure on our funding. It must be a result of his manipulation, your efforts are all we have between failure and survival," Ben replied, "and he'll know that. You must be very careful. We know that he'll kill to get what he wants."

2

A week before Clare left London for Vancouver, Rebecca Rosslynn had been walking slowly, at the edge of the Pacific Ocean, along a beautiful beach near her home, in Sydney, Australia, barefoot and relaxed. Sometimes splashing in the wash of the waves, and sometimes admiring the changing sea, and its reflections of the rising sun.

The freedom of the breaking waves captivated her, drawing her toward the vast beauty of the sea, she longed to fade into its cool frothing wake.

Her cell phone interrupted her reverie.

It was Matthew Clement, the head of Binnett, an unusual and unexpected honor.

She turned to face the shore, head bent into the slight offshore breeze, with her back to the waves, one hand covering an ear, so that they could hear each other.

Clement asked her if she was going to a Vancouver conference on operations performance.

"I wasn't planning to," she replied as she walked slowly away from the sea.

"It's an important forum for us and the industry, a good place to meet people."

"Yes, I went to it last year," she replied warily.

"This year it will be even more interesting," he said, and went on to tell her that the conference was going to involve discussions of problems similar to those she'd faced in Ngami, the previous year, when she had been involved in the rescue of the Ngami process plant, and the older linked mine."

"I'm not keen, Mr Clement."

"Your experience will help me and others avoid similar situations."

"I'm not sure I want to relive the exercise. Failure came too close. Support was missing and physical danger was being covered up at the highest level. How am I going to tell a hall full of people about that?"

"Yes, it was a bad situation. That's why I'm doing what I am, and I sympathized with you, and with the people who were threatened by the fraud, and those affected by the violence, but we are in business, and a huge part of our revenue was at stake. We simply had to do what we did. What's important now is that we must be prepared to face similar difficulties."

"I understand that," she said, thinking, "I wonder if you can imagine how terrible it was for me?"

"This unstable economic environment is likely to cause similar difficulties, both for us and others. Your experience would definitely help others manage similar circumstances."

"I suppose I should help," she answered unenthusiastically, "have you spoken to my manager?"

"Yes, I've spoken to him, and he suggested I should talk directly to you."

"I wasn't planning anything too intense here. I'm tired and still stressed from the Southern African exercise, but I'll help if you need me." The whole time she was thinking, "Do I really have a choice?"

"Thanks, Rebecca. I also need to talk to you about my plans for the firm and your place within it."

"I see. Okay, Mr. Clement."

"I'll look forward to seeing you there."

She turned and walked back toward the sea, to stand for a moment at the limit of the breaking waves, looking out on the Pacific wondering at its ever-changing color. It now seemed to be more turquoise than blue.

Seagulls darted in and out of the waves, adding to their reach.

She turned again, to continue her walk home, sticking to the wet sand, left by the waves, for better traction. It was firm and crunched under her toes.

Stopping for a while before leaving the beach, she looked back and could see her intermittent tracks, a set of bare footprints, disappearing where fresh waves had washed. They were, she thought, almost a reflection of the lonely trail that her apparently spectacular career had followed. Too much left behind, and all of it temporary.

It was early in January, mid summer in Sydney, the day was going to be warm, in the thirties, and she had not fully engaged herself in the new year. It had been a quiet holiday season and she had been looking forward to a few days away from the busy city.

Rebecca thought about what Clement wanted her to say about Ngami, and the unpleasant exercise there. Since whatever she said would involve the hard pressed Ben de Bruin, and the Ngami tribe, she wondered if she should perhaps call him and, discuss what Clement was planning, but eventually decided against the idea.

***

As the time to leave for the conference drew near, Rebecca's concern for the de Bruins overcame her reticence. She called Ben, thinking that; since the previous year's problems were behind her, and the original Ngami project had been pulled back from the brink of disaster; the family's problems would also have become less serious.

He asked if he could call her back.

"Hello Ben," she answered the returned call, "how are you?"

"I'm okay but our new mine is in trouble."

"Why, Ben?" she asked awkwardly, surprised at the tumbled out comment, immediately regretting the impulse that had led her to contact him.

"The number of problems that have held the work back is unbelievable. We're being pressured by the bank and don't have the contacts needed to deal with them, so now we can't finance the ongoing work because we need to have the new mine's capability certified."

"Odd at this stage?"

"That's putting it politely. Your call could not have come at a better moment. We need a certified confirmation of the mine's reserves, and it would be simple for you to provide one."

Rebecca was certain that her firm would not consider certifying anything for the de Bruin's, after the previous year's exercise, however much anyone understood their problems, answered, "Have you spoken to Michael Anders? He would be able to help you."

Michael Anders, younger than Jack, was the heir to the majority of the shares in a major corporation, GVN, he had taken responsibility for running the Ngami process facility and its linked mine, as managing director, when he had forced his cousin Jack to relinquish all his Ngami responsibilities, to prevent a disaster.

Michael had left Jack in his other role, as managing director of GVN corporation, until Michael was ready to take over that role, to avoid bad press publicity. However Jack had not been phased by the setback, he had intensified his plans to step into the ranks of the very rich, at the expense of Michael, the de Bruins, the Ngami tribe and GVN itself.

Michael, although heir to a fortune, had had an isolated childhood. His mother had been killed when he was a baby, in one of the political power struggles for the states of central Africa. She had been in an aircraft, shot down by a terrorist SAM missile along with his brother and sister. His successful and well-respected father, who owned most of the shares in GVN had been severely affected by this disaster and had become withdrawn, reclusive, guiding Michael's development, but not being close to him.

Since completing university, Michael had been working on the corporation's many sites learning operations practicalities, from both technical, and front line management perspectives; and, despite his impending inheritance of the bulk of GVN's shares, he was not familiar with board room politics. He had only recently returned to the Johannesburg corporate office, to prepare for the planned take over from Jack.

No corporate network, no power base, and few contacts among Johannesburg's power brokers, left him in an exposed position.

Ben answered Rebecca, "I've tried talking to Michael, but he's such a quiet bloke, and lately he's even more distant. He almost seems to be drifting."

"That certainly won't help," said Rebecca, awkwardly. "But Ben, if we get involved, we will face intense opposition, in Johannesburg, as we did before."

"I wouldn't ask if we weren't desperate," said Ben. "Couldn't you simply write a report based on what you know? Without the extra finance, we're finished."

"I'm fully committed to Binnett. I can't possibly do anything on my own, especially for that exercise. Everything I do depends on what Binnett wants, and their approval of work related to Ngami is really unlikely considering what has happened there. I will speak to our branch manager about what you need, but there is very little chance they can afford to get involved."

"Binnett is heavily involved with GVN," he replied, feeling and sounding petulant.

"It's not something that's just happened. Neither I nor the international firm know the full extent of the South

African branch's involvement with GVN or anyone else for that matter."

"I appreciate that, Rebecca, but I don't know what else we can do."

"I wish I could help, Ben, but it's out of my hands," she answered, trying to concentrate on what her manager, Chris Bain, had said about the situation, the previous year, "The failure of the de Bruins is just another collapse in a world full of such tragedies, and it simply means a victory for someone else. The fact that this victory will take a fortune with it is just another statistic in a hard world of similar failures."

Rebecca knew that what Ben faced was not as simple as economics, and did not honestly believe that it should be treated as such. Clearly he, and the others were again dealing with a deadly threat, based on the greed and dishonesty of Jack Anders. She also thought, as did, it seemed, Clement, and his associates, that with new technology, globalization, and effortless communication, similar efforts were an international problem. This meant that turning her back on Ben was much the same as turning her back on a reality. One that she knew was far more important, than her own self-interest. However she could not overcome her self interest. She tried, instead, to console herself with the knowledge that she had not followed the malevolent path that had been laid out for her by Jack during the previous year's problematic exercise. She had stood by her technical decisions in Ngami, to the detriment of her own position, and she had been forced to walk away from the assignment.

***

After saying good-bye to Rebecca, Ben sat wishing that he had gone to the Vancouver conference himself.

Michael Anders had suggested that he present a paper on their reasons for choosing mechanized mining systems for the new development, saying that this form of 'advertising' would benefit the reputation of the partners in the platinum venture.

However one calamity after another had meant that he had too many things that he was running himself. If he left the site at this point he would be would handing the game to the forces they were facing. He simply did not have have the time to go. He sighed and shook his head. He was desperate, however he factored the situation.

The successive setbacks, in the new work, together with the dangers inherent in the existing project were slowly overwhelming him.

***

The flight attendant on Rebecca Rosslynn's journey from Australia to the Vancouver conference was impressed by Rebecca's manner and by her appearance. During quiet moments she had glanced at the beautiful consultant, and wondered at the possible importance of the elegant woman's thoughts. By appearances Rebecca could have filled almost any role. The consultant's soft accent and unassuming attitude had completed the impression.

Rebecca was dressed in a casual, dark blue outfit that accentuated her striking, bluish-green, almost turquoise eyes. Her face was framed by dark, chestnut-colored, thick, and beautiful hair that almost seemed to glow in the reading light of the aircraft. Her elegance was a result of precise attention to detail as much as nature. She considered that appearance was as important in achieving support and cooperation as was capability.

Rebecca was not thinking about world affairs, or great themes, as the flight attendant surmised. She was plagued by doubts about the conference, and thinking about what she could, or should do, to help Ben and the other partners in Ngami. The hours of flight passed slowly, and she struggled to rest.

A man across the aisle, from her, smiled pleasantly at her when she got up to go to the toilet.

He was thinking how attractive the woman looked, though she seemed somehow unapproachable.

She returned the gesture, politely and confidently, and turned away.

3

After talking to Rebecca in Vancouver, Ben went to a celebratory gathering, being held because the older Ngami plant had achieved a record production run.

Clare's e-mail, saying that she had failed in her latest attempt to find extra finance, one they had thought to be their best hope, arrived shortly after he reached the venue.

He walked into the hall, asked for a beer, and picked up a bowl of snacks, then found a chair, slightly behind, and to the right of the bar, away from the crowd.

He sat down to read the message.

Depressed, by her negative report, he sighed and closed his eyes.

Anne, one of the technicians, who worked on robotic aspects of the new project, was walking toward the bar as Ben was reading the message, and saw his reaction.

He was slumping in his chair as he put the phone away.

He took a few potato crisps from the bowl, nibbled slowly at them, washed them down with a sip of beer.

He looked, to Anne, more like a sad creature from a children's storybook than the dynamic person she knew.

The nibbling grew slower and more deliberate; and she thought that his face reflected a series of unwanted prospects.

Ben's frustration with the message was all the more intense because the major work on the new mine was done and production had started. The new platinum mine's financial model required output that was close to planned targets. These were not being met and this had unsettled their bankers. Nothing he had said to them had convinced them that they should extend the loans.

As she watched Ben, Anne wished she could do something to help. She liked and trusted him, as did most of the workforce, but she had no idea what she could do. She was as worried about the future as were the rest of the community. She decided to ask him what was wrong.

Ben's phone rang, and Anne hesitated.

He answered it almost anxiously, and she heard him say, "So, Peter, what's the verdict?"

Ben was perspiring freely, as she was herself. The air conditioner was not handling the extreme heat. It was midsummer in southern Africa and they were near the equator.

Peter Connell, Ben's friend, associate, and the chief engineer, was telling him of another calamity; some of their newly commissioned machinery would not produce continuously in the hot weather.

Ben said, "Surely that's ridiculous, Peter. Why the hell would they make anything that sensitive?"

"Heavily loaded machinery generates heat. This equipment is designed to work in confined spaces, so each part is made small. Small motors in enclosed spaces, being used at high loads, represent a challenge for designers, they must not have been designed to cope in these conditions," Peter answered.

"So what's that mean for us?" Ben said.

"Each loader might need upgrading," Peter told him.

Anne heard Ben say, "That's going to be the end of us. We've designed the bulk of the ongoing development around those machines. They are a big expense even without us having to pay for extra requirements."

Not a complex comment, but one that seemed to Anne to represent the death knell for all of their dreams. Anne was not sure how bankruptcy would affect the money they were owed in bonuses by the company, but her very least concern was one of not wanting to have to start over somewhere else.

The original, and now proven, project was separated in distance and ownership from the new platinum source being developed by the de Bruins and the Ngami tribe, without the support of GVN, the third partner in the original project. The older project needed the new ore source for its own viability.

Ben said dully, "Thanks anyway, Peter. Keep me informed."

She walked determinedly to where he sat, and said, "Hi, Ben. Why are you hiding down here on your own?"

He looked up and tried to smile, shaking his head and sighing.

"There are a few things worrying me."

"We are celebrating though?"

"We're out of the woods on one front, but we need production and profits from the new development. How are you managing, yourself?"

"I'm fine. Thanks largely to your efforts."

"We've a way to go, Anne," he said, sadly, "Further than most people realize." Then he stood, and said awkwardly. "Still, I don't want to monopolize your time. You get on with your evening. I must leave early."

"Oh," she said awkwardly.

As he walked through the door to the surrounding veranda, the outside heat hit him like a blast of hot gases from a furnace. He was silently cursing Jack Anders for his greed, and himself for the mistakes he had made. Somehow he had to work out how to move forward. He sighed as he turned away from the stairs that lead into the night and made his way toward the end of the veranda at the corner of the building.

Anne had been hurt at Ben's reticence. She returned to the bar to attract the attention of an attendant and asked for a glass of champagne.

The courteous young woman handed her a cold glass filled to overflowing, condensation dotting the outside and reflecting sparkles of light.

Anne thanked her graciously, and was rewarded by a shy smile, "Always a pleasure to help you, Mme. Anne."

Anne moved back toward the group she was with.

"What's the matter, Anne? You're looking a lot less happy than you were a minute ago," said one of the men.

She shook her head and tried to smile casually. She could not think of anything to say. Her thoughts were filled with a consciousness that this might be the last Ngami celebration.

4

Rebecca disembarked at Vancouver International Airport, collected her luggage, passed quickly through customs, and went to hire a vehicle, feeling drained after the long flight from Sydney.

Once she had completed the paperwork, the pleasant car hire company representative handed her the keys, with a large smile, and said, "Your car is the red one out front."

She thanked him warily, and walked out to the car park.

It was a clear winter's day—crisp, clean, and refreshing—but the cold was intense. The fresh air washed away some of her jaded feelings. A brilliant sun and the clear blue sky framed the snow-covered mountains.

The only red car was a latest model Mustang. Not a luxury she would have presumed to pay for at her level in the firm.

Concerned that she had not read the contract properly, Rebecca turned and marched back into the building to tell the official that he had made a mistake.

"There's no mistake, that's the car I've given you. We don't have a standard, so you're entitled to an upgrade. I thought that driving a Mustang would make your stay more exciting," he said, his smile even more dazzling than before.

Rebecca, feeling awkward, surprised, and cheered by the simple gesture, thanked him and went back to the Mustang. The Canadian's smile and warmth had reminded her of a friend, that she had met in Vancouver on a previous assignment and he smiled to herself at the memory.

She packed her luggage into the Mustang and drove off, toward the city.

On the way she slowed several times, to better appreciate breathtaking views.

The problems of the de Bruins and Ngami kept surfacing as she drove, as did the thought that they had been forced into the new development, by Jack Anders' unbridled attempt to hijack the new ore source.

She also worried about Ben's reply about the reason for the lack of production, "Odd mishaps, random, unpredictable, far too many of them," seemed an echo of the previous year's nightmarish events.

"Could they have been deliberately triggered?" she had asked.

"It seems unlikely, although there were common threads—often they occur late at night, some are not reported for hours, hard to pin."

She drove on, firmly rejecting the need to care about the de Bruin's problems. Her profession was her life. The power of the vehicle was an added distraction. As she accelerated away from a stop she felt happy to be free for the rest of the day.

***

Ben strolled along the veranda, after leaving the hall. He could think more clearly in the fresh air. An outdoorsman, a farmer, and a geologist; he was happier outside.

He reached the end of the lighted veranda, and stood looking out into the shrubs that led into the darkness, and mystery of Africa. The shadowy shapes of the surrounding range of kopjes were just visible in the night.

He sighed and took a deep breath, enjoying the scents of Africa, of wood-fires, the bush, and its inhabitants;

trying to think his way through his impossible situation. Ann was right, he needed someone to talk to, but he could not allow his guard to slip. Site morale was too fragile.

He sighed again and sipped at the beer.

The extent of his involvement, in the day to day management of the original operation, and now the new development, had grown exponentially in the last few months.

He had had to adjust from a life as an enthusiastic geologist living in the bush, whose main task was micro managing every statistic and every find, to full-time management of two complex projects, in which micro management was rarely the best way to achieve good results. This had come about as Michael Anders had left more and more to him because of his need to keep up with what was happening in the GVN headquarters in Johannesburg.

"Rebecca is really the only practical way to getting finance, she knows what we have here and has a high credibility with the type of people we need to influence," he thought, "if only something would pull her away from the obsession she has for conformance with the propriety of her firm and its agenda," but he sadly realized this was most unlikely.

His thoughts drifted to Africa's tradition of dreamers and achievers, van Riebeck, Rhodes, Barnato, Burnham, Baden-Powel and many others; and tried to tell himself that they too had been desperate at times.

"I can't allow Jack Anders beat us, I must find a way to get through to Rebecca, there isn't any alternative," he took another sip of his beer and began to compose an email.

5

The Vancouver conference was due to start the day after Rebecca arrived in the city. So the free day provided a perfect opportunity to revisit some of the places she had enjoyed during her previous assignment. She drove the Mustang briskly through the city, across Lions Gate Bridge toward North Vancouver, to the base of Grouse Mountain. Fully appreciating its power and balance.

That assignment had been a turning point in her life. It had lasted for two years, and she and her Canadian friend and colleague, Hong Kong–born Ian Mui, had spent many happy days in the city and in its beautiful surrounds.

Grouse Mountain had been one of their favorite spots, both for skiing and hiking. He had taught her downhill skiing on its slopes.

She parked near the sky ride, looked up at the cable cars, and thought of Ian; then of her first trip up the mountain before she had met him. It had been autumn and the car was nearly empty, so she had been able to look out from different windows, to take in the many aspects of the beautiful city. The pines, spruce, and larch seemed to stretch their verdant green needles toward them as they glided upward.

At the top station, she had wandered about, soaking up the sunshine and scenery, to eventually stop at a point where she could see some of the many peaks in the ranges behind Grouse.

That experience faded into dreams of the times she had spent at the same spot with Ian.

She had given up the plans they had made, together, to further her career. She sighed and wished, as she sometimes did, that she could break from the tight discipline that had held her in its grip for so long. She closed her eyes for a few minutes, shook off the feeling.

The weighty subject matter of the next day's conference began to fill her mind, after half wishing that she had taken the steps that she and Ian had planned. Not having heard from him in a while, she thought of phoning him, but decided that too many years had been lost.

She started the Mustang and returned to the highway, again enjoying the car's effortless power, and drove on, between the coast and the mountains, past West Vancouver, to Cypress Provincial Park; with its memories of fun, snow, and warmth, of cross-country skiing. The cross-country tails had been terrifying because of the terrain. They weaved through a wonderland of towering trees and snowdrifts, among high valleys and streams, in the mountainous terrain.

She arrived at the car park, turned the engine off, looked up at the mountain, and pictured the past. Like many others, Rebecca had spent more time in the snow than on skis while enjoying cross-country trails on Cypress. During her first few outings, the easy routes had seemed so difficult that they could just as well have been a remote part of Alaska. The snow had then been new and soft or she might have never have kept up her efforts to master the cross country equipment. She had only subsequently learned that the snow conditions could vary considerably. On a later visit, a fall, on to the icy packed snow, had resulted in a painfully grazed face.

Her falls had been eased by Ian being there to help her. On each outing, they had ended at the Hollyburn Lodge. The warm, steamy atmosphere, the smell of hot bread, cheese, and coffee, the tastes, the heavy wooden tables, the benches, and the people had complimented many melted cheese rolls and cups of delicious coffee. Looking up toward the cross-country skiing trails from the car park, she thought of the graceful figure Ian had cut, as he telemarked, making other skiers look like amateurs. His cross-country skiing ability had been outstanding.

Eventually, after restarting the Mustang, she brought her thoughts back to the present and drove slowly down the mountain and on to Horseshoe Bay. There, she made her way into a familiar restaurant overlooking the ferry station to have lunch.

"How can I help you?" asked the smiling, good looking young waiter.

She ordered a coffee, then opened her tablet computer to glance through her e-mail, finding a summary, from Matthew Clement, of the aspects he wanted to convey at the conference and recalled her horror at what Jack had done the previous year; one person's death, Ben de Bruin's near-death experience. And eventually there was the closely averted flood, which would have killed an entire shift of the operations workforce.

"That the apparently impeccable Jack Anders was, by far, the most dangerous aspect we faced is difficult to comment on," she thought restlessly, "The extent of the situation, might be easier, though."

***

The previous year, Jack Anders, acting managing director of GVN, had employed her through Binnett to carry out a technical study to justify shutting down the original, supposedly hopeless, Ngami project.

She had been given no inkling that the reason Jack wanted the Ngami project closed. Rebecca had carried out the initial part of the work she had been employed to do, which was to assess the project's capabilities. She had found the prospects for the project were bad. However during the second part of the assignment, when she was supposed to institute the project's closure, she had realized that this would provide a huge, low-cost, opportunity for Jack Anders, bankrupted the de Bruins, and caused large losses for the Ngami tribe. She had, by then, also realized that the project was not beyond rescuing. This meant that the closure of the Ngami, would leave Binnett open to charges of fraud.

She had clashed with the South African head of Binnett, a close associate of Jack Anders, over the conclusion, and had been removed from the project.

***

Gazing out over the ferry terminal at Horseshoe Bay, Rebecca could see further than was usually the case at this time of year. The view of the greenish blue of the inlet, framed by deep-green conifer clad mountains, capped with snow was even more beautiful than she remembered.

The Bowen Island Ferry docked, as she watched, and she decided to spend a few hours visiting the island, where she still owned a four-acre block of land.

She ordered, and then finished her lunch, at Horseshoe Bay, then drove up Nelson Avenue, toward the highway, along the longish loop to the ferry station.

After crossing the ramp onto the ferry, she parked and walked up to the deck where she stood for a while, soaking up the atmosphere, before finding herself a seat from which she could see the mountains during the crossing.

There was a short wait before the ferry pulled away, to plow through the deep, dark, blue water. Flocks of gulls provided a noisy, wheeling escort.

Her wonder at the beauty of the short crossing was rekindled, and her concerns vanished, as the spectacular green and white backdrop of the snow-covered mountains on the mainland slipped behind the ferry's wake.

Disembarking on Bowen Island, she glanced out to the left, thinking that the blue waters of the bay seemed an unlikely looking home for a huge numbers of eels, that, she had been told, made the estuary their home, and shivered at the thought.

Ben's problems, and the help he needed with Ngami, intruded into her thoughts during her drive across the island. However the journey was too much of another step along the lane of her past for her to give them much thought, and lost moments, with Ian, regained her attention.

Twenty minutes after disembarking she parked at Bowen Bay where the block of land, that she owned, was located. She stood looking at it, from the road, before making her way around the extensive, undeveloped, green-treed block. The view of the Strait, from parts of of the block, was beautiful and she spent more than an hour thinking about how best the investment could be developed.

The return journey took Rebecca back across the verdant island, to the ferry, the mainland, Lion's Gate Bridge, through Stanley Park, and ended when the sun was low on the horizon;.

She drove up to the Westin Bayshore where the concierge took her car keys and bags.

Rebecca strolled through the expansive foyer to register.

The view from her room was even more spectacular than those in the parks and on Bowen Island.

The evening unfolded its shadows as she sat looking out on the changing colors of the spectacular landscape: Lions Gate Bridge, behind Stanley Park, pointing to

Sentinel Mountain, Grouse, Cypress, and the ranges behind.

The mountains slowly turned purplish black, as did Stanley Park on its peninsula.

Yachts bobbed at their moorings. Floatplanes changed color; from pinkish white, to mauve, and then purple, as they drifted down to land with plumes of spray trailing behind them, in the shadows cloaking the water way.

She thought again of the places so filled with her memories, of Ian; skiing, cycling, and hiking. She remembered with happiness the seasons; spring, and its kaleidoscope of flowers, especially the cherry blossoms. Summer flowers, autumn leaves, salmon swimming up seemingly impossibly small streams to spawn, and winter with days like the one just past, and others darker, filled with rain, or blanketed by huge snowfalls.

She dreamed on, of what might have been, as the mountains and light slipped away into dusk, and the water in the harbor turned black.

Eventually she closed the curtains and turned on the lights, to read for a while.

6

Ben's email arrived while Rebecca sat reading, at the desk in her room.

It said, "Hi Rebecca, I desperately need your help. Can I phone you?"

She sighed, she really did not need Ben's problems; but after a few moments she replied, with a message asking him to call her on her cellphone, about the help he needed.

Her phone rang, she hesitated, then answered to hear Ben's greeting; and said, somewhat untruthfully, that she was pleased to hear from him. After exchanging pleasantries, she told him she was in Vancouver for the conference, which they had discussed during their last conversation, and asked, redundantly, how they were managing.

"Not at all well, Rebecca."

"I gather from your message that things are bad?" she asked.

"Yes, infinitely so. Clare still hasn't had any success with finding a source of funds, and now we've had another major failure with high costs."

Embarrassed by Ben's desperation and by her fear of helping him, she continued, "Ben, I would certainly do anything I could, but the same restrictions I faced before will apply. Nothing has changed for me. GVN is a major client of ours."

"A short study on your own would be all we'd need."

"Too many contracts prevent me from doing private work. I need permission from Binnett's management to do anything on my own," she said, then, hesitatingly, half biting her lip, added, "but I'll talk to Clement, the head of the international firm, who's here, about the idea. Can you send me all the details?" adding almost without meaning to, "There will also be people here who might help with financing. If you could get here yourself, it might be a good idea."

It was a small step, and as much as Ben had hoped for. He answered with a measure of relief, "I can't get there, Rebecca. There's just too much to look after here. I've only just taken over myself."

"Surely Ben, there must be other competent people there? What about Peter and Jeffery?"

"Michael is spending almost no time on site, Jeffery and Peter are good, but there are over a thousand people working on production and construction, and both of them are completely tied up with the problems in their own areas of responsibility."

"Well, Ben, you are the one who wants the help."

"My sister Clare has the details with her. I'll call her and ask her to drop her efforts to find financing in London and get to Vancouver."

"That would be fine."

"Thanks very much, Rebecca."

"The conference starts tomorrow, so Clare would need to leave soon."

"Thanks Rebecca."

"If I can, I'll try to get Clement to meet her for dinner. He will certainly know people here who can help, if only he could be given a push in some way," Rebecca's relief in doing at least something for the de Bruins was transmitted in her tone of voice.

***

Standing alone in the call booth, stuffy with the smell of his perspiration, Ben's hope had been revived, but he could not help wondering why everything had to be such a battle. "Perhaps it's self-inflicted, aiming too high. We've had to go forward though or go under. Perhaps simply bad luck," he realized though, that the truth was that he had managed to achieve more than any person he knew. One step at a time. Their chances had improved, to fail now would be terrible. They desperately needed this bad period put behind them.

He turned to walk back along the veranda and down the stairs into the African night, toward the unique smells of the continent, and away from the community hall and its representation of industry.

Clare would have to be told what he had arranged, and he had no doubt about how annoyed she would be. He decided that it was too late to phone her and that he would leave the call until morning.

He drove to the company guest house, which was situated in a quiet part of the village, parked on the verge and was surprised to see someone on his own in the otherwise deserted suburban street, in the shadows opposite the house. He made his way through the front door, wondering if he should call the security section, or the police and decided it was more likely that the man was one of their people than anything else. Robbery and violence were uncommon in Ngami.

Ben showered, made sure the air conditioner was not overloaded by open windows or doors and looked out onto the street.

The person seemed to have gone.

He walked back to his room, made sure his automatic pistol was within easy reach, turned off the lights, climbed into bed.

Then he heard a noise at the back door. He sprang out of bed, readied the gun, and tiptoed through the dark house to the back door. There was nothing to be seen and no further disturbance. He went to the door, opened it and searched the the lighted yard. Someone crouched into the back room's doorway. Not sure what to do, he decided that the person looked too frail to be a danger. He swung the door open his pistol pointing into the yard.

What looked like a child ran through the side gate to the front garden.

Another homeless child he thought and went to the front window to see a small figure disappearing along the lighted street.

Ben returned to the bedroom, after locking up again, and, and lay there, for what seemed hours, before falling into a restless sleep.

His sleep was filled with nightmares. The terrible history of his people back through time haunted him. He was South African to the core, but firmly indoctrinated by his grandfather in the history of his French antecedents, partially Huguenot, partially Catholic. Their history in France was something he longed to explore, but had never had enough time to even check on, because his own life had been so busy.

Ben bore other hidden scars and fears. He had lived, as a small child, through the worst of the last Boer Republic and had been involved in several unbelievable horror stories.

The de Bruins were from a farming community. They had only recently extended their interests to make up for the shortfall in financial capability of the farm by using Ben's find of the ore deposit in Botswana.

The size of the family's farm was not enough to take them into the category of independent farmers. Their property, like many others of that era, had been in a precipitous state when he was a boy.

While many people from similar backgrounds had given up and joined the industrial society, as employees, the de Bruin family had decided to remain self sufficient

His brother, with Ben and Clare's outside support, had managed the farm well, rebuilding it into a reasonably successful small Cape winery. They had developed a niche for their wines after South Africa had emerged from the shadows of apartheid and the income from the winery now provided a living for his brother James's family but was not enough for him or Clare to stop work.

There was more than enough room in the old family home on the farm. It was big as well as historic, but Ben and their sister, Clare, still needed a separate income.

He had also contributed to the work on the recovery of the farm while using his qualifications as a geologist to supplement the farm income.

Many years had passed in field exploration while they were working to rebuild the farm. This exploration had led to the first and second platinum discoveries in Ngami.

During the development process they, with their partners, the Ngami tribe, had approached GVN to provide the management and technical expertise needed for the initial project, in exchange for a holding in the venture. The first of the platinum discoveries had been developed, with considerable ongoing difficulties. The second was the one now threatening to bankrupt them and during the last year Ben had been forced to spend more and more time on the site as the GVN management had become more of a problem.

He thought affectionately of his sister, Clare. She had been a huge help, always so much of a support, feminine, yet so very independent.

Her mission to London had been made possible by her taking her annual leave.

Ben woke once during the restless night and lay thinking of his limited options. He decided that he had to go to Johannesburg to see Michael Anders, while trying to go back to sleep.

7

Early on the day after he had spoken to Rebecca, Ben woke and lay in the predawn silence, trying to think what else he could do to save their investment. Eventually, not having solved any aspect of the quandary, he got up, and showered.

After a quick breakfast of muesli, he decided he needed to speak to Charles Obenta, who represented the tribal interests, both in the original project, and, in the new platinum venture. He phoned the Ngami tribal chief to ask if they could meet.

Ben and Charles had started the development together, before involving GVN. The relationship was not free of problems, because, although Charles's people were on good terms with the de Bruins, there were dissenters.

Whether those who opposed them did so for financial reasons, or because of political ambitions was not clear to either Charles or Ben.

Charles was waiting for him in front of his office when he arrived, and they walked through the office gardens to discuss their options. Charles turned on his phone's speaker system and set it to play music loudly enough to confuse any long-distance monitoring of their conversation.

Ben explained the latest problem with the machinery and detailed the family's closeness to failure,

Charles answered warily, "So suddenly?" adding, "We don't have any reserve funds that could be used to help, I think I've enough influence with the government in Gabarone to get some support from them, but it might put your difficulties on show in Johannesburg, and you've said before that any weakness on that front will finish you. Can't Michael Anders help?"

"I'm going to see him, but he's even more remote than usual at the moment."

"It is odd how, since he took the place of his cousin as managing director of the site, he's faded away. At first was terrific, but as you know, he's seldom here now.

"I wondered if you knew why," said Ben.

"I don't hear much from him."

"I don't want you to do anything Charles. I just wanted to ask you, before I see him, if you know what's happening with the GVN politics and particularly, Michael Anders. I need to know why he's never here."

"He doesn't discus what he's doing with me."

"On the financial side of things I'm sure he's wealthy enough to support our need for extra finance."

"I don't know, Ben, I've no idea about the corporation's politics, or his, for that matter. I know his cousin is ambitious, but Michael was definitely in control when he took over here."

"You didn't have much contact with Jack, did you?"

"No, I didn't. I hardy know him. We left them alone, having involved them for their expertise, I, like you thought that that was enough. What I of course know is that Jack is very sophisticated, and dangerous, in image and in reality."

"So Michael has not discussed GVN politics with you?"

"Not really," said Charles. "When he took over, last year, from Jack, as managing director of the original development, to prevent the disaster, he told me a bit about Jack. He was busy whenever he was on site after that, and he's a quiet sort of person. The whole GVN enterprise, not just Michael or Jack, is a a puzzle to me.

"They are, and were, experienced operators, and our taking them on as a part in the project, to fill the managerial and technical skill gap that existed in the beginning, seemed a brilliant move. Their involvement gave us access to technology and management ability."

"We couldn't have guessed that Jack was dishonest."

"It sure is hard to deal with," said Ben.

"So to sum it up, Ben, I don't know about Michael. You'll have to talk to him yourself."

"It's so darn difficult, at long range, with these security people working for Jack's private company."

"Crazy. We must get them offsite too."

"Very difficult."

Ben arranged to go to Johannesburg. Rather than attract attention by leaving Botswana on an unscheduled trip, he telephoned the specialist who had treated him after he was nearly killed during the previous year's problems and told him about the recurring headaches he was having.

The specialist agreed to meet him at Oliver Tambo International Airport, near Johannesburg that morning, and Ben booked a seat on the first flight. He then phoned Michael, and they spoke for a while about machinery failures and production.

Ben said he was going to be at the Oliver Tambo airport that morning to see his specialist there. He asked Michael if he would like to meet him for coffee,

They agreed to meet at the airport.

8

The next morning, as Ben had waited for his flight from Ngami airport, he sent the message to his sister Clare, in Mayfair, about going to Vancouver, to meet Rebecca.

The flight to Johannesburg was short and uneventful. Then disembarking at Johannesburg, Ben noticed a site security agent coming down the stairs behind him. Repressing his annoyance, he walked slowly on toward the coffee venue, where he was to meet Michael Anders, by way of a bookstore, as a check on his suspicion that the man was following him.

The agent stayed near him.

Ben spent several minutes looking for something to read, thinking, "Why the hell should someone trying to make a success of his life be so victimized by a corporation," knowing full well that it was not something that he could avoid, and, knowing that no amount of philosophizing was going to help, he walked on irritably, to the coffee shop.

He accepted the table he was offered, in the quieter end of the shop, sat down, ordered a coffee, and waited until the security agent had found a seat. Ben then moved, choosing another table, in a noisy spot at the other end of the shop, and made it quite clear that he had seen the man, by waving to him.

He called the waiter and redirected his order for coffee.

Sitting, sipping the high quality brew, he tried to read the novel that he'd bought.

Michael arrived within minutes.

Ben told him that they were being watched and pointed to the agent.

Michael shook his head. "Crazy bloody situation. Do you think he can hear us?"

"No, he can barely see our table, and I've made it obvious that I've noticed him."

Michael nodded and asked, "How can I help, Ben?"

"The new project is insolvent."

"So suddenly?"

"I've told you we've been missing our targets. Too many small failures have limited production and our income, taking us to the limit of our funds. We need to refinance, and because the machinery now seems incapable of doing what it was specified for, we look like having to upgrade it, at the same time."

Michael knew about the revenue shortfalls, but, considering the huge potential and the progress already made, had not thought they would present too much of a problem. "Surely you can just talk to the bank?" he asked.

"No. They're adamant that we must stay within our existing overdraft limit or they will foreclose."

"That's odd, it's a very valuable asset, who are your bankers?"

Ben gave him the name of a well known bank.

"Jack has an association with several of the directors there," said Michael.

"I might have guessed that."

"Another bank?"

"We're trying, but now with the extra expense of the machinery, we are in an even worse position."

"What about the manufacturers? They agreed to carry the development costs, didn't they?" Michael asked.

"The contract says that we will share the machinery, research, and development costs," answered Ben.

"Clare went to London about refinancing didn't she?" asked Michael.

"Yes, but she's not come up with anything so far."

"Why, I wonder?"

"The money markets are very tight, and everyone she's spoken to wants an independent statement of capability."

"Get surveyors in to give you one?"

"We haven't had enough time, it would involve more than survey work. They need technical assurance as well. I've tried to get a capability statement from Binnett, but they are not keen to do anything that will conflict with GVN."

"I don't know whether such a statement from them will, or will not, contribute to GVN's objectives," said Michael.

"But, you are taking over the corporation, aren't you?"

"I'm supposed to be. What about asking Rebecca to do something on her own?"

"I've asked her," he said and went on to explain her point of view, and then asked, "Do you have any connections that would help?"

"I'm not sure what I can do, Ben."

"Perhaps some form of a guarantee," Ben tried again.

Michael was silent and Ben's discomfort grew.

Eventually Michael said, "Hell, Ben. It's very difficult for me at the moment. I've been put into a corner myself. I'm going to have to get clear of Ngami."

"Why?" asked Ben, sounding desperate.

"Since I've got back to head office, from Ngami, Jack has made my role in Ngami seem naive. Using that, he's building an image of me as ineffective and so, instead of steadily taking over in GVN, I'm being marginalized."

Ben did not answer. This was not what he wanted to hear. It was almost worse than the financial problems. Michael was their only certain ally in GVN.

Ben did not know what to do, he hesitated, they had to have Michael's effective support, just to keep the overall project on the rails. If that slipped away Jack would win, without the financial obstacles the family faced.

The waiter interrupted their conversation to take their orders.

"What's happened?" asked Ben.

Michael explained how, feeling exhilarated by his success in Ngami, he had returned to Johannesburg to take control of his supposed inheritance, the GVN corporation.

"That's what I thought you were doing."

"I ran into a series of barriers. At first petty issues: My personal assistant, who I hardly knew anyhow, since I have only been back from the overseas postings for a short time, had been dismissed, and had not been replaced. Then my parking had been given to one of the financial investigations people. There were other small things, like not being put on mailing lists and not being included in some decisions."

"Sounds irritating."

"Yes, but it's got steadily worse. I tried to deal firmly and coolly with the odd problems and issues, but there were so many that I began to look like I was running around foolishly, worried about petty annoyances."

"But if you own the majority of the GVN shares...?"

"I'm heir to the majority of the shares, and before going to Ngami, there had never been any question about my taking control of GVN."

"What else happened?" asked Ben.

"Jack has set me up to look responsible for last year's Ngami problems. Because GVN is a very significant public company, the directors are in the vanguard of the city's top people. There's no quarter given when they sense incompetence. They could and would block my appointment if they felt I did not belong in the role."

"Why would anyone think negatively about you?"

"After I managed to get him clear of Ngami, Jack retained his role as acting managing director of GVN, and used it to publicize my direct involvement in the Ngami work, implying the work I've done was altruism gone wrong."

"But, you've done a brilliant job in Ngami."

"No one in Johannesburg knows anything but what Jack implied or said."

"And that's enough to cripple you?"

"If it were shown that I was incompetent, they couldn't legally allow me to take the position of managing director, or for that matter as a director."

"But, surely, you would have some say in their appointments. They'd owe you something, surely?"

"Not at the moment. My father is the major shareholder. I don't own enough shares to influence much and, anyhow, proven incompetence is a barrier to even the mighty."

"What about your father?"

"Jack is his protege. I'm something from his past."

"Hell. Is there anything I can do to enlighten them? Present a report? Write to a paper? Something?"

"Not in time, Ben. I just can't help you in any way at this point without Jack putting a spotlight on the effort as naivity."

Ben sat in silence for a few moments and then said, "You stepped in to prevent a disaster for GVN. Because of you, Ngami is in full production."

"Not your new venture yet, and no one on the board knows what actually happened. If you cannot manage your finances, it confirms Jack's implications, that I supported you for the wrong reasons, and so I'm not suited to taking over the corporation."

"What a nightmare. It sounds like we're not much more than a threat to your own position?"

"I'm afraid there's no better way to put it, Ben."

They parted and Ben phoned the airline after Michael had gone, to book himself onto the next flight back to Ngami.

The specialist, who had arrived as Ben and Michael finished talking, said, after they had greeted each other, and Michael had left, "Let's carry out some checks to see if we can find out what's causing the headaches."

Ben agreed, and, after Ben booked his return journey to Ngami, they made their way to a medical emergency room in the terminal building.

The specialist carried out a few basic tests and asked Ben to get a blood sample to him, using the Ngami clinic.

Ben e-mailed Clare, while he waited for his flight, to explain that they had no chance of getting any support from Michael. He also suggested that she should contact Rebecca the moment she arrived in Vancouver.

His flight was eventually called, and he walked, listlessly, out to the aircraft, thinking that at least the flight from Johannesburg to Botswana was always a pleasure.

The plane left on time, despite a looming storm, and he watched the smoggy, industrial area around Johannesburg fade below, to be replaced by the rough bush and red, rocky country that made up the northern parts of South Africa, an area that had been traversed often in the last two centuries by Nguni impis, wagon trains, and both settler and British armies. Yet, from the air, much of it still looked completely unspoiled.

They skirted a thunderstorm and crossed into Botswana, and Ben thought how fortunate its people were. It had been well managed by the Tswana people and their leaders. Botswana had some of Africa's most successful developments and yet the unspoiled nature of the fragile country remained intact.

He put his head back and closed his eyes. Even if the direction taken in the development of Ngami was idealistic, he still felt quietly pleased with its planned positive contribution to the country and its people.

9

The storm clouds overhanging the 'City of Gold' were dark, churning, promising a drenching that would refresh its polluted air.

Thunder accompanied its arrival.

Dust and litter filled the air, and swept into the wind tunnels formed by the tall buildings.

People were avoiding outdoors, threatened as much by the dust and flying litter, as by the storm.

As Michael drove back from his meeting with Ben his mood matched the weather. As far as the de Bruins getting more finance went, he was certainly in as bad a position as Ben. He wrestled with ideas about how to help anonymously, and decided that, since he knew and trusted both Rebecca and the international head of her firm, his best approach to helping Ben would be to back Ben's effort to recruit Rebecca Rosslynn to prepare the capacity certification that they needed.

After he got to his office, he sent Rebecca an email, asking her if she could find a way to work on behalf of the de Bruin's, explaining that it would benefit him as much as them. He also explained that, because of his awkward position, he did not want to have his part in the exercise publicized.

After sending the message, Michael stood, and walked across to the window.

He leaned against the sill and looked out on the city thinking that his not expecting the onslaught had been reasonable; a result of a continued presumption that, since he was the heir to the GVN corporation, his position was safe.

He knew that he should have been more careful, but he was not sure how, "If only I had more contacts in the corporate world," he thought. His training on remote sites in Europe, Australasia and America had provided him with no clues about how he should manage Jack and whoever he was working with, and this could almost be anyone; the amount of money involved could pay for a lot of dishonesty, if it were even thought of as such.

He gazed out of his office window, across the city, feeling desolate.

The door between his office and the outer reception area was open and Jane, his new PA, could see Michael's tall frame, hunched, with his hands against the window sill, looking like a tower that was about to crumble.

Michael was so withdrawn that he had not fully noticed her. She anxiously watched him and wondered if she should ask for a transfer. Moving to the doorway, she said, "Could I get you something, Mr. Anders? Tea or coffee or anything else?" She had only started that week and was unsure of herself, barely able to conceal her nervousness.

Michael looked up and smiled, warming the atmosphere. "Sorry, Jane. I'm having a bad time, and I've been almost ignoring you. Yes, please, can you get me some coffee? And bring a cup for yourself, we need to get to know each other a bit better."

She smiled with relief, and had to force herself not to rush when she went to get the coffee.

When they were both holding mugs of steaming coffee—aromatic and freshly brewed, sitting at his desk— she nervously asked if it was Ngami that was bothering him.

"In some ways Ngami is in a much better situation than it was. The World Bank has extended the loan for the project for an additional twelve months," he replied.

"So you're no longer so worried?" she said, noticing the piercing blue of his eyes.

"No, I am worried."

"Why is that?"

"All the original difficulties are still in the background."

"Is there a production problem?"

"It's under control in the original project, but not put to bed. For instance, the crews working in the endangered areas have to check on the water inflows and on rock movements all the time, because there is still a threat of a failure that could injure and kill people and, at worst, even flood the mine."

"What can they do about that?"

"They use cement injection, and bolting to strengthen weak points in the rock structure—both of which are expensive and time-consuming. The production from the area is planned to be reduced by the new development."

"Is that where the problem is?" Jane asked.

"It's not happening as it should."

"What does that mean?"

"The ore supply, for the reduction plant was complemented during last year's exercise, by a new mine. It's owned by the two partners that we have in the main project, the de Bruins and the Ngami tribe. The deposit is good and has a great deal more platinum than the original orebody, so it's very valuable, but it needs separate ongoing finance."

"Why is that a problem?"

"The de Bruin family's personal finances, which are supporting the new part of the project, need perfect management."

"And they're not well managed?"

"They are, but there have been a series of problems that have cost too much, occur too often, and are often not properly explained."

"Surely the new work can't be sabotaged?"

"There's no proof of that. Just late night calamities, a normal part of mining. But in Ngami, there are too many of them for comfort."

"So the production is down?"

"Not constant, so they have a cash flow problem. Cash flow uncertainty means that there's always a chance of losing their finance."

"Can't you help them with that?"

"I wish I could, but there's too much going on here that prevents me from becoming involved in their financial problems."

"What's happening here?" she asked.

Michael, thinking that he should be careful with what he was saying, answered, "Innuendo and politicking at my level is hard to handle."

"I see."

He nodded, saying, "Too many things that can go wrong."

"Can I help you in any way?"

Michael hesitated, then said, "I need to deal with it myself."

"I'll help in any way I can."

"Thanks very much. I've enjoyed talking to you. That's been a help in itself. What about you? What were you doing before?"

"Oh, there's not so much to tell. I've been working in Europe for a while, for my father's company."

"Which company is that?"

"It's not well known. They import foods and essences."

He asked a few more questions about her background before standing to go to the company library.

"Thank you, you've also made my role more worthwhile by involving me," she replied, awkwardly, and went back to her desk.

Following his conversation with Jane, Michael went to the library and looked up the archived information he was interested in and then went for a walk, down the fire escape and into the lobby. He was feeling more relaxed. Talking with Jane, about the quandary, had helped. He decided to go to the coffee shop that was on the ground floor and met Jack and the financial director in the foyer.

Jack barely acknowledged him, and the financial director followed suit.

Michael stopped for a moment, feeling insulted, and then checked his feelings. This was no time for self pity, the rude greeting could only mean that he was running out of time. He had to act. He thought for a moment about his email to Rebecca, and decided he needed to do more than that; Binnett was the only option he had. He decided to talk to the international head of firm, Matthew Clement, who he knew from work he'd once done in Boston, New England.

He changed direction, went out into the garden, that was enclosed by the foyer glazing, and phoned Clement.

"Hello Matthew, he said, sorry about the sudden call and so early too, but I urgently need your help," and he went on to explain what he was facing.

"So, you're certain you're going to lose control of your inheritance?" Clement said after listening to Michael's story.

"That's definitely happening."

"Leave it with me. I'll talk to Rebecca. We seldom come across anything like this."

"The problem is time. I feel almost foolish, but I just don't know what to do."

"I appreciate the urgency. I'll think about it and see if we can come up with, but its going to be difficult. Our branch in South Africa is very successful, and not interested in confronting GVN, who, in the person of your cousin, are their best customers."

10

In London Clare had decided to begin her journey to Canada soon after Ben's call.

Having put her phone away, she glanced at her image in Purdy's, Mount Street window, and thought that she looked as stressed as she felt. "Perhaps Ben is exaggerating," she said to herself, realizing, as she did so, that he was not. The high stakes, that were sought by Jack Anders, would easily justify their killing her.

She called her date, and said, "I'm not going to be able to get there Derek, I've got to do something for my brother. Can we have breakfast another time?"

"Where are you going?" Derek asked.

"I've been asked not to say."

"Well, I don't suppose I've much choice," he answered, "Where are you going anyway?" he repeated.

She was surprised that his tone of voice indicated so much annoyance, she hardly knew him after all, his annoyance, rather than disappointment, was not at all what she had expected from the awkward big man. His dark and lithe manner had made her feel she was dealing with some one caged, in need of kindness, "I can't talk about it, but I've got to attend to something that's come up," she answered.

Derek stood and moved away from the table as he spoke, "I'll come with you," he said and walked to the entrance of the little shop.

He stopped on the pavement outside, looked up and down South Audley Street, trying to see her, thinking that she must be only minutes away.

She was; just out of sight, in Mount Street.

"No, that's not possible now, I'll call you when I get back," Clare answered.

Derek walked back into the tea room.

Other customers, put out by his loud telephone conversation, his awkward clothing, his stressed mannerisms, his caged, almost dangerous seeming manner.

Derek while returning toward his seat, was thinking that he needed to call his employer, and noticed the nervous stares of the other patrons. He changed direction, walked out of the tearoom, and made a call to van Zyl, who ran the international security firm for whom he worked.

When he got through, Derek told van Zyl that his mission to side track Clare had failed.

"So where is she?" asked van Zyl.

"I don't know. She wouldn't tell me," Derek answered, looking toward Purdy's.

"Derek, you must stop her. You only have to keep her out of the way for a few days."

"She didn't arrive. How was I supposed to do anything about that?"

"As I've told you, time is the issue with this job, my associate and I will loose out on a huge deal if the woman is not sidelined for at least a week."

"I understand, but I can't do anything without knowing where she is," he answered.

"I'll see what I can find out about her plans."

Derek was as on edge as his tense manner suggested. He desperately needed the fees he'd been promised to get Clare out of the way for a time. This was because he had accumulated huge gambling debts, to totally dangerous people. People who did not accept non payment.

Having no reason to go anywhere but his hotel, he walked back toward it, past Grosvenor Square, away from Purdy's and Clare.

Clare had spent a moment thinking about what to do. Her passport was in her handbag. She also had a laptop and the papers and reports she needed, for an afternoon meeting. Having no reason to return to her apartment, other than to pick up clothing and toiletries, she decided to go directly to Heathrow.

She turned, and walked toward Park Lane, where she caught a taxi, thinking about her planned meeting with a prospective financier that afternoon.

She phoned the contact, and explained that she had to go to Vancouver. They agreed to an alternate date.

At Heathrow, as Clare walked slowly through the extensive duty free shopping area she thought that the tempting array of goods seemed to be mainly intended as gifts for loved ones. She sighed feeling terrible about Derek. He had made her laugh with his quick, unusual wit. He had been considerate too, despite his obviously stressed manner, he was uncluttered, rural, real. Their chance meeting the night before had been a pleasant respite.

"Pretty appropriate to be meeting Rebecca. The pair of us have too much experience in business and too little in life," she thought sadly.

Pausing before the security check, she decided to phone Derek, to tell him she was at the airport and about to leave for Canada to attend a meeting there.

"Well, I'm amazed," Derek replied, his voice expressing a now surprising degree of hope, after hearing where she was going. "You miss our date and the next thing, you're on your way to Canada. Where in Canada?"

"It was a sudden problem. I'm not supposed to talk to anyone about it."

"Who says you shouldn't talk to me? Where are you meeting them?"

"Derek, I don't want to discuss it. Can't you try to understand?"

"Clare, this is like movie stuff. If you don't trust me—"

"I can't discuss it, Derek. Please try to understand. I'll contact you in a few days," she finished, feeling much worse.

Wishing she had not called him, she put the phone away, and walked on, increasing the length of her stride, feeling disappointed by his pushiness.

After passing through the security checks, she boarded the aircraft, found her seat, and fastened the seatbelt. Feeling uncomfortably hot after the cold of the London morning, she worried that she smelled sweaty, and wished she had bought some perfume in the terminal.

Derek phoned van Zyl after the conversation and told him what he had found out about Clare's plans.

"No idea where in Canada?" asked van Zyl.

"No, I pressed her, but she didn't give me any hint."

"Go to the airport and I'll call you."

Van Zyl's next call came while Derek was still in the taxi on his way to Heathrow.

"She's going to Vancouver. I'll get you on the next available flight," said van Zyl.

"How do you know that she's going to Vancouver?"

"There's a conference that the people from Binnett and several other similar firms are holding. It's about their work in primary industries and will involve key figures from industry."

"Where in Vancouver?"

"At the Westin near Stanley Park."

"What do I do there?"

"I'll book you into the hotel under the false name in the passport you've been given. Use it for the flight, too. Get rid of the woman, then get back to the UK. I'll book your return flight for late this evening. If it's not safe to do so, you must remember to change the booking."

Derek silently caught his breath and thought, "Get rid of her. That's not been mentioned before. I was supposed to get friendly with her, get to know her movements, stop her meeting anyone for a few days, and now I have to kill her?"

He had been delighted to get the well payed job. The money would have covered his debt. He had realized there would be some degree of violence, intrigue, danger, bending the law. "But kill Clare?" he though desperately, "Hell, what have I taken on now?"

Derek's life had been out of control for several years.

"You want me to kill her?" he said.

"Derek, this is not kindergarten not even the bloody army. You are not part of the good guys doing the king's will. You are being paid a lot and that will now be doubled, your work is critical. Get your perspective sorted out, or get out of there and I'll replace you."

"What do you want me to do?" Derek answered.

"For now, you need to consider how to stop her in any way you safely can. She has to be taken out quickly."

Derek had a tough military record. He had however been court-martialed for being caught out in a offense related to his gambling and drinking.

He hesitated again, trying to think of how to answer without committing himself.

"Do you want me to send someone else?" van Zyl snapped.

"No, no, I'm on my way. I do need to think, though," Derek said in his too-loud voice, and, to van Zyl, his too-common accent.

"Don't think too much. Phone me when you get there," van Zyl said.

"What about some sort of weapon?"

"There's no one I know who can help get a weapon to you in the time. You were in the special forces. Use your initiative."

***

Van Zyl arranged a backup, angrily telling his British contact, "I thought we should be careful with such an obviously flashy loudmouth."

"Van, your requirement when I recruited the man, was to sideline the woman here. You didn't say you wanted to kill her on another continent."

Van Zyl said, "Please make sure of what you're doing now or we will not have any further use for you."

The international security company that van Zyl owned in association with Jack Anders was based in Southern Africa. There were huge opportunities in the strife torn continent for people willing to go beyond the boundaries civilized behavior.

The recruitment to cause Clare's failure had had to be rushed, so it had been arranged through British associates.

Van Zyl contacted Jack Anders to explain what had happened.

Anders said, "Van there must be no mistake about this. She must not be allowed to speak to any financiers in Canada or the United States. We have the Ngami partners where we want them now. They can only survive if they come up with the money. I have no way of influencing financiers in America. I don't even know anyone who does."

Van Zyl said that he was certain that, between the backup arrangements and Derek, they would prevent her from meeting anyone.

***

Derek, on his way to Vancouver, was more desperate that he could remember and coldly afraid. He finished a good many more drinks at the airport, and during the flight; and he was feeling a little slow by the time he arrived.

After disembarking, he ate a handful of spearmints, hired a car, and drove toward the Westin Bayshore along Cambie Street. He looked out on the mountains that formed the city's backdrop, thinking, ruefully, that his last trip there, ten years before, had been a holiday with his family. He sadly thought how his then little girl had then been talking to him as her big daddy bear.

How far he'd fallen. He sighed restlessly and tried to shake off the hopeless feeling.

He stopped at a hardware store along the way to find something to use as a weapon. Firearms were too complex to acquire at short notice. He looked at an axe and decided it was too obvious and difficult to handle. A hammer would be too unusual in a public place. He then looked at knives, but again, they were difficult. He would have to get too close with a knife, and without being recognized. He walked along the aisles and found something labeled as a finial fence post; sharp-pointed, solid, light enough to lift and swing. It could be mistaken for like a long ski pole or a walking stick, then continued his journey to the hotel.

Clare had told him how much she liked being outdoors, and that she walked or ran when she was stressed. Derek guessed that, after the complex morning, the bright weather and Stanley Park would draw her out.

11

On the first day of the Vancouver conference, Rebecca woke early, some hours before Clare's plane was due, and went for a walk through Stanley Park, to its western boundary.

While she was standing there, next to the Strait of Georgia, looking out over the ocean, an American family with several excited children paused next to her.

One of the family's little boys decided that he liked her.

Trying to leave, she found herself being pulled into his world, physically. He had grabbed her skirt and was holding her back.

She extricated herself from his grasp and carried him back to his group of siblings, who seemed not to have noticed his departure.

She walked away, back to the hotel, wondering at the maternal feeling that she had so suddenly experienced.

When she got back to her room. The more detailed explanation of what Ben needed for the Ngami project had arrived, as had Michael's request, that she should help Ben.

Her experience of the heir to the GVN Corporation had been gained at meetings and in short conversations and she did not fully understand his situation. She only knew that he would inherit a majority of the shares in the iconic GVN and had presumed that this was something that would not change and that it guaranteed his role in the corporation.

The conference was slowly coming to life when Rebecca arrived downstairs. She found a seat near a window with a view.

Clement, the distinguished, gray-haired principal of her firm, whom she had met several times before, in Sydney joined her.

His ruddy, character-filled face increased her feeling of involvement as much as did his pleasant greeting.

After a few preliminary pleasantries, she explained Michael's message, about the contacts she had had with the de Bruins and about Clare being due in Vancouver.

"Michael Anders has told me about the current situation and asked me for our help in dealing with his cousin at the corporate level."

"What does he want you to do?" she asked.

"He's not sure, but he urgently or, I think more accurately, desperately, needs help. It seems that his cousin Jack has used his role as acting managing director of GVN, since Michael took control of Ngami, to discredit him. So Michael has become vulnerable himself. It seems they are blaming him for the problems at your favorite site."

"The opposite is definitely the case."

"I know, and I've decided to do what I can to help."

"What are you going to do?"

"After he called, I invited some financiers, with whom I sometimes work, to have dinner with us tonight. Can you get Clare de Bruin there?"

"That would be great. I'd hoped you could meet with her for dinner anyhow."

"I'll contact Michael Anders about a telephone hookup. Now, let's get this presentation ready."

"Okay."

"Thinking about the latest circumstances, and Michael's position, I've decided that we need something more direct than I had originally planned. Rather than backing me up, you should give the keynote presentation using your experiences."

"The work I did is confidential, isn't it?"

"Yes, don't refer to any particular site or set of people. The main thing I want put on record is how you were pressured to wipe out people's investments."

"I'll do what I can."

"We don't need too much detail."

"So you want an overview of the situation and the outside control attempts, to give the conference an idea of what's happened and the pressure I was subjected to?" said Rebecca.

"To be an example of the dangers in our type of work. You need to show the dishonesty, with a fairly clear exposition of what has happened. Don't tell them that the client is in Africa. We can review it at lunch time."

"How long is the presentation to be?"

"I'll introduce you in about five minutes. You speak for a half hour, then ask them for their opinions on how they would deal with the situation you've faced. That will take another twenty minutes. I'll finish by explaining that the exercise is still causing major problems."

Rebecca stayed where she was and used the intervening time to prepare the talk.

Sitting at the coffee table, her brow clouded, she began preparing the presentation.

A waiter, a vacation student, could see she was stressed, and almost offered to help. Realizing that it was not his place to do so. He settled, instead, for making sure that she was well attended.

A slide show was ready in time, and Rebecca ran through it with Clement.

They made a few changes, and he told her that he had asked the organizers to record her efforts.

In the conference, Clement introduced Rebecca and explained that, rather than present a history of difficulties, he wanted to involve the conference in a current disaster, that had arisen through a conflict between commercial reality, terms of reference, and ethics.

He then handed the stage to Rebecca.

In her presentation Rebecca described what had happened to her, and to other key players in the conflicted assignment in Ngami.

Clement thanked her after the conference and said he would see her at dinner. "Are you able to bring Clare de Bruin?"

"I haven't heard from her."

"Where is she?"

"I don't know. I'll check with reception."

"If this contact of mine decides to help, they'll be able to provide long- and short-term financing."

"I'll get back to you," she said, and headed for the front desk.

***

Clare de Bruin had arrived from London after the conference had started.

She spent some time wandering around the impressive facilities but, tired from the nine hour flight, and the fact that the actual Vancouver time was only an hour later than that at which she left London, and too on edge to really appreciate much. She did not feel like doing anything sedentary, so she decided to go for a walk, left the hotel and headed toward Stanley Park, passing near where Derek Jones was waiting for her.

Derek started the hired car and followed her.

She turned right at the end of the street and walked briskly toward the thousand acre Stanley Park.

12

When Ben got back to Ngami from Johannesburg, he was still feeling hopeless and unhappy. He was as much a victim of the immense powers at work in the world as was Derek the lost northern English fitter and turner, who was stalking Clare.

Ben, however, had no intention of being forced into the wilderness.

Peter Connor was watching, from the Botswana side of the custom's barrier as Ben pulled his bag irritably from the heavily loaded baggage trolley, thinking how driven Ben was—not so much by extraordinary ambition, as by what was almost a crusade to achieve some destiny. He worked to build a future, one of hope and improvement for everyone concerned. Putting more effort into the development of, and for, the future than anyone Peter had ever met.

They had been friends since their first meeting, and neither of them had many other confidantes.

Other than his wife and family, Peter tended to keep to himself and so did Ben. However Ben had never married nor formed any permanent relationship. Peter had never asked him why, but assumed that his work in remote spots, combined with running the de Bruin family business, must have been the reason.

Peter watched Ben turn away from the baggage trolley, tall, well-built, tanned by his outdoor life and naturally fit from his work. Tenacity and strength showed in every line of his posture.

A rather sloppy, but well-dressed, young man casually pushed Ben out of the way to get his own case.

Ben turned, clearly intending to give the slob some of his own medicine.

Peter saw what was coming, but could do nothing to physically stop Ben. He called out "Ben!" so loudly that people turned to stare.

It was enough to stop the geologist, who, surprised by Peter, turned away from the sloppy man and strode across to where Peter was standing.

"Hi, Peter. What are you doing here? I was expecting my assistant to collect me," he asked through the opening.

"I needed to talk to you, urgently."

"What's the matter," asked Ben."

"The loaders are a disaster, they are definitely going to cause a loss of production. We've finished the tests, and they definitely need upgrading. The thermal ratings of the motors are too low."

"Why would they build machines that cannot perform their designed duty when they're for use in a hot environment?" asked Ben in a deflated tone of voice.

"They have such a low profile that every bit of space is valuable," answered Peter. "Small space equals small heat dissipation, and to that we have to add that the ambient temperature during this heat wave could be higher than they allowed for in their design."

"Surely it's always been hot here—they should have allowed for that."

"Not as hot as this. The temperatures this week are breaking records."

"What are you going to do?" said Ben.

"Reduce the work that they are doing. We need to know exactly what the limits are, and then work within them but it will mean a reduction in production."

"Limit the production? That's not a good idea."

"Until we carry out the changes."

"How are you going to do that?"

"I need to get exact information. We'll need that anyhow, if anything is going to get redesigned."

"Sounds like it'll be expensive."

"Not to get the information, but I must have accurate data quickly. Paying for modifications is another story. I need to go ahead with the investigative work right now, and that needs your approval. I'll do what I can without using outside help."

"Okay," said Ben.

"How was the trip to see Michael?" asked Peter as they drove off.

"Hopeless."

"Why?"

"He's in some kind of bind with GVN. Jack's making things difficult for him."

"That's a disaster in itself."

"To put it mildly."

They arrived at the workshops to find a supervisor and two technicians.

Ben listened to the supervisor's commentary and asked if the manufacturer's representatives had agreed with him.

"Yes, they agree and will look at upgrading the machinery. The agreement we have is for development work on the machinery to be a joint expense."

After they left the workshops, they walked toward Peter's vehicle, and Ben turned to him, saying, "Telling them we'll pay them and actually paying them are not the same thing in this case."

"I don't envy you, Ben."

"No, I don't suppose you do, although we're all involved and heavily committed. I'm not working alone, that's for sure. We need to know how much these machines can produce. We'll have to try to increase production in the old workings to keep overall production up, or increase the amount of traditional mining that we do here."

"We can't increase output from the dangerous area in the old workings," said Peter.

"We have to improve our rate of development."

"Back to the loaders, the quickest way to get a measure of their capability will be to drop production by forty percent and see if the problem goes away, and then pick up in ten percent jumps until the machines overheat."

"Okay, Peter, good luck, and let me know how things are going. I'll ask Jeffery if he will look at reducing our dependency on the new machines."

"Go back to the old way? Winches and so on?"

"I'll just ask him to look at it—I'm not happy with being so dependent on something that's having problems."

Ben's vehicle was parked near the workshop. They asked for the keys from the tool store man, who had been looking after the vehicle.

Ben accepted the keys and, after parting, drove away from the workshops toward the surrounding bush.

Ben's black mood had been taken on by Peter, who was worried about his own commitment to the project. He'd changed from consulting for a successful partnership —first to independent consulting, then to hands-on management in the shaky operation. As things now stood, the moves had never seemed less like good decisions.

Ben was in native bush a few moments after leaving Peter. The country surrounding the area where the new equipment was being worked on was largely uninhabited by anything but game.

He looked around at his surroundings as he drove to see Charles Obenta, to tell him about the meeting in Johannesburg. Hoping more than believing, that their struggle, against corrupt corporate manipulators, to develop an ecologically neutral source of one of the world's rarest elements, was not too unequal,

Charles was in his office when Ben got there, and stood to greet him. "So, my friend. What's happening?" Charles asked.

"The new mining equipment is still acting up. It definitely can't handle the heat."

"Can't say I blame it. Even though I was born here, I'm really uncomfortable this summer. I don't know about global warming, but I'm sure we've got something happening in Botswana."

"They've had to ration water in England, there seem to be fires everywhere and then there are so many floods. There's something odd about it all."

"And the Arctic is melting so fast that the Northwest Passage is an open waterway."

Ben pointed outside, and Charles showed him into the pleasant garden, more green than most because it was watered from a borehole.

"What else Ben?" Charles asked when they were outside.

Ben told him about the lack of any help with finance and that Michael Anders was facing rejection by the GVN board.

"Not good?"

"Really not good," said Ben. "It sounds as though he's got no chance of surviving."

"And you?"

"We're very shaky. I've contacted Clare, and she's going to Vancouver. There's a faint chance Rebecca Rosslynn can help her."

"In Vancouver?"

"There's a conference there that will involve people that can help us find finance."

"Binnett have been bad news for us though?"

"That's true, but Rebecca is okay."

"There is something else Ben, a group of the miners has gone on strike, you need to talk to them."

"What is their problem."

"It's this internal faction that is working against me, and I think with the security section, meaning Anders and van Zyl. You are the only person who they will listen to. They have been so impressed by your efforts that you might be able to solve whatever it is that they want sorted out."

13

Clare emerged from the hotel, soon after Derek had found a parking space, with a view of the pathway that led from the hotel.

He knew that she was supremely fit, an accomplished proponent of unarmed combat, and a long- and short-distance runner. Although he was strong and fit, he decided that she would easily outdistance him if she ran.

He started the hired car and followed her.

She walked to the street corner, turned right from Bayshore Drive, into the road leading toward Stanley Park.

Derek followed slowly.

The street ended in a dead end for cars, with access to the footpath leading along the foreshore for pedestrians only, so he turned the vehicle around, toward West Georgia, planning to intercept her in Stanley Park where the footpaths crossed Stanley Park Drive. Once there, he waited below the bridge, near the intersection of the cycleway and the paths from the city.

Clare arrived soon after he had stopped and walked toward the yacht club.

Derek, still feeling disoriented from the many drinks he had managed to consume on his journey, and from the heated car interior, wondered if he should drive over her while she was on the road, and decided, fuzzily, that she would dodge the car. He shook his head and wished that he had not had so much to drink.

As Clare neared the information kiosk in the park, Derek caught up with her, pulled ahead, and parked. He stepped from the car, took out the rapier-like final post, made sure no one was around, and moved quickly toward Clare to stab her.

She saw him, recognized him at the last minute, and shouted, "Derek what—" Her fitness and unarmed combat training were at a peak, and she moved enough to avoid being killed by the sharp rod. She was very fast, and managed to hit the big man in the solar plexus.

He tumbled forward, gasping for breath.

"You bastard," she said, and kicked him.

His mouth filled with blood, but his concentration improved, and he was strong, not long away from his own full-combat training. He was heavily built and taller than Clare, but nowhere near as quick on his feet.

His longish black hair was standing out making him look wild.

Derek, wheezing, scrambled up. He could see Clare was hurt. The makeshift weapon had gashed her arm. He hesitated.

Clare, in a blur of pain and confusion, rubbed her wounded arm.

Derek gathered his wits and flew at her with the finial post, using it as a rapier.

Clare saw his intention, grabbed at the implement, pulled Derek off balance, and kicked him again, this time in the groin. He was in agony but the shock was so great he overcame the pain and managed to pull the weapon back. He stabbed at her again, this time firmly finding his mark. The makeshift weapon penetrated her chest near the shoulder.

She tumbled forward onto the pathway, bleeding from her chest and arm.

He pulled the weapon free, then whipped her with it, knocking her out.

A woman, who had not noticed, ran screaming at him.

Derek, still struggling to get his thoughts straight, ran back to the car, started it, turned it, and drove at Clare.

The woman jumped aside.

Derek hit the curb, but had misjudged its alignment. This caused the car to swerve, buckling the wheel and upsetting the steering. He missed Clare.

Realizing that something was damaged, he decided to leave the scene.

He turned the vehicle away and drove off.

The woman, who had come to Clare's assistance, found that her breathing was shallow. She stood, ran to the information kiosk, and asked them to phone for help.

She then walked briskly back out, carrying some clean cloth, followed by others who wanted to see what had happened.

A man tied a tourniquet around Clare's arm, using his belt, while the woman who had witnessed the assault helped stem the flow of blood from the shoulder wound, using pressure and a cloth.

Clare moaned. The flow of blood onto the pavement slowed and was eventually stopped.

A cab had pulled in, the driver jumped out and offered the use of his taxi to get her to the hospital.

"It would be better to wait for an ambulance," said the man who had tied the tourniquet.

"I've radioed the police," the cab driver said.

The journey from the park to the hospital took about twenty minutes, and the highly trained hospital staff took Clare into the operating theater within minutes of her arrival.

The police arrived while Clare, still unconscious and breathing shallowly, was being wheeled into the theatre.

They asked how she was, and were told that she would be lucky to live.

Derek was sick to his core at what he had done. The damaged wheel made the car's progress erratic, and there was a thumping feeling in the steering. He stopped for a minute when he thought he was well out of sight of the information kiosk to see what had happened. The tire had not deflated, but the wheel was slightly buckled. He jumped back into the vehicle and headed toward North Vancouver. He phoned base and explained what had happened, slurring slightly.

"So she can't talk to anyone?" asked van Zyl.

"I'm not sure, but she was bleeding a lot. I'd say she's pretty far gone for sure."

He was told to go to Abbotsford, dump the car in a shopping center car park, and wait there.

"The car's a bit wobbly. Don't know if it will get there."

"Wobbly?"

"I hit the curb, quite hard."

"Where are you?"

"On the other side of the Lions Gate Bridge from Stanley Park, near a river."

"Hang on."

It was cold, and Derek was miserable.

"There's a shopping center there, Park Royal. Drive into the middle of the car park and leave the car. Go inside the center. Are your clothes all right?"

"Bit dirty. It'll clean up."

"Someone will contact you."

Derek parked near the shopping center and walked toward the building, feeling sick to his core, he'd killed people in Afghanistan in battle but nothing had felt as bad as his attack on Clare.

Van Zyl phoned Jack Anders and told him what had happened.

"So she can't talk to anyone about finance. The conference is over tomorrow, but, Van, we need to make sure of that. Try to keep in touch with her condition."

"I will, but the people I'm relying on are complete unknowns."

"We lost out at the last moment last year. Please make sure you don't loose the ball. Go there yourself if you need to."

"It will take two days for me to get there," said van Zyl.

"There are billions at stake. Surely you can come up with something."

"Look, Jack, it's been less than a day since she changed countries. It was not me that stuffed your efforts in Africa. It was Michael."

"Ben de Bruin should be dead."

Van Zyl bit back any further argument. Jack was his partner in the security firm, but he was certainly not anything more than part of a meal ticket. Van Zyl could recognize the danger of Jack's naked drive, his power, and his existing and planned wealth. At least well enough to control his tongue.

"I'll keep a close watch on what's happening," van Zyl finished.

Two back up agents arrived after a long wait.

They arranged a new set of clothes for Derek and when he was cleaned up, they took him to the airport and saw him out of the country.

They then went back into the city, to take a room for themselves in the Bayshore Hotel.

Derek arrived back in London, was paid the agreed amount for his work, paid his gambling debts, and walked the streets of London for days trying to think how to find work and deal with the future.

He sat on a bench, still feeling sick about Clare, he shuddered in horror at how the waters of his life had flown away.

Ten years earlier had seemed a different planet, one where he had been a proud father husband and skilled tradesman working in a factory in Manchester.

After being retrenched, he had tried to survive by taking part time work in service industries, but his size and manner were not gentle and he was not suited for customer service, of any type.

Eventually, as his hope and pride diminished during the months after the factory had closed, and the work had been shipped offshore, Derek began to gamble, this and drinking led to greater desperation.

The efforts get enough money to support his frightened wife and their three children changed to efforts to cover increasing dept.

Then, he had joined the special forces, partially to escape the first debtors and partially to find a place in society.

He sat next to the Thames, shook his head, and sighed thinking of his ex-wife, and his children, now teenagers.

He cried dry tears of hopelessness, then looking into the distance, he bit back the self pity, pulled himself together and tried going over, again, his list of potential jobs.

One, among them, highly paid, that he had missed earlier, jumped out at him. It was oddly titled, and the more careful examination showed that it described someone exactly like him, someone was needed, with his trade skills, in a remote place.

Perhaps he could disappear. He read it again and felt a spark of hope, he thought he would meet the requirements.

He headed back to his room to apply for the position, and in so doing, began a journey toward an even greater nightmare.

14

The hospital had given the police, investigating the attack on Clare, a card key for her Westin Bayshore room.

They took the key to the hotel and the person working at reception ran it through their system to identify Clare.

They were told that she had left Rebecca Rosslynn's name as her contact.

The police asked to be put through to her.

Rebecca went cold when the police told her what had happened.

She was at the front desk in minutes, looking as frantic as she felt. "What actually happened?" she asked the officer.

He explained and asked what her relationship with Clare was.

"The company she represents is hoping to employ the consulting firm, that I work for, to assess an operation of theirs," she said.

"Have you any idea why anyone would want to injure her?"

Rebecca hesitated. She did not want to bring the complicated corporate story into the sphere of a police investigation. The Canadian police were certainly not people with whom she wanted any difficulties. She could not see how they would deal with the corporate aspects and answered, "Their company is involved in a high-risk mining venture, and they are very vulnerable. I suppose that it's possible that there is some connection, but you would need to ask her those questions yourself. At the moment, I'm simply arranging meetings for her. Surely a mugging is a more likely explanation?"

"There is no indication that this was related to business, the way she was attacked was personal, the woman who found her heard her shout, "Derek," as he attacked her.

"A personal attack?"

"As I said, it sounds like it was. Do you know anything about her personal life?"

"Nothing, and she's only just arrived in Vancouver. I've known her for some time, and we get on well, but it's been a business relationship. I do know she's a very committed to her family's business and doesn't have much of a social life because of her work."

They had no other questions to ask, thanked her and left a contact card.

After the police had gone, Rebecca phoned Matthew Clement. "Clare de Bruin has arrived, but she's been hurt."

"What happened?"

"She was attacked in Stanley Park."

"Good grief, where is she now?"

"In hospital."

"Where?"

"North Vancouver. I'm on my way there now."

"Will you call me if you find out anything else."

Rebecca said that she would.

Ed Chalmers, the Australian general manager of a small mining company, who had helped Binnett in Ngami after Rebecca had been withdrawn from the site, was also at the conference. He had been in the foyer when the police arrived. Hearing the exchange between them and the receptionist, he had decided to wait for Rebecca.

After the police had left and while Rebecca was talking to Clement, Ed phoned the hospital to find out how Clare was.

They told him that she was starting to come round.

Rebecca noticed him when she heard him talking and walked over to where he stood.

He told her that the hospital had said Clare was recovering consciousness.

"Should we go and see her?" she asked.

"Yes," he replied.

About two hours later, Clement met Rebecca and Ed in the hotel's foyer as they returned from the hospital.

"How's Clare doing?" he asked after greeting them.

"We asked the person in charge if she was going to be okay, and he said it was too soon to say. She still wasn't fully conscious when we left."

"What happened?" he asked.

"Someone attacked her in Stanley Park."

"A mugging?"

"We don't know. Apparently she recognized the person who attacked her."

"At such a critical stage that's the worst possible luck for the de Bruins."

"If it was simply a random attack. I wonder if it was not planned by Jack Anders."

"Surely not."

"Coincidence seems less of a probability."

"If this relates to their problems, then this Jack Anders affair is far worse than anything I dreamed of finding, I've never dealt with personal violence against a client before, and haven't heard of anyone else doing so either."

"I've told you that it's bad," said Rebecca.

"And, if your guess is right, then it seems that you weren't understating the lengths to which they're prepared to go."

"There is no doubt about their malevolence. It's how anyone normal deals with it that worries me. What about dinner with the financiers? Should we cancel or delay it?"

"This mugging is going to make it very difficult to get anyone to part with money. It's a long shot anyhow," Clement answered

"I know. Perhaps Ed could talk to them about the project. We don't have to tell the people what happened to her."

"That's an idea, he's had some involvement with the site, hasn't he?"

"He's familiar with Ngami, so he'll be able to provide the de Bruins's perspective," she answered.

"The banker has said that he's bringing a mining expert, who they want to consider the practicality of the Ngami project, so Ed, with his mining background and knowledge of the project would help," said Clement.

"Ed wouldn't know what the latest extraction plans are, but technically he understands what they involve. He could carry the discussion at least as well as Clare."

"Good, so we'll go ahead with the dinner."

Clement phoned Michael Anders after his conversation with Rebecca.

Horrified to hear of the attack, Michael said, "If Jack is behind it, it's the worst thing he's done. I can barely believe it's not just a mugging."

"She called 'Derek' when she was attacked."

"Not a mugging then."

"It's really hard to believe. But that's not the reason that I called you. I've arranged for a meeting with potential backers for Ngami. Rebecca and Ed Chalmers will put the case for the de Bruins and you need to attend, using video conferencing."

"I'm worried about being involved myself. Jack could use any hint that I'm helping to drive me further into oblivion."

"Your life is tied up with them," Clement replied. "You must attend or they won't get the money."

"No matter how much I think about it, I cannot accept an attempt to murder Clare. If my cousin and his associates are involved then they have to be stopped. I'm in a difficult position with the politics in GVN though."

"You're right about stopping them. Seeing Rebecca's presentation today about the efforts of that cousin of yours to bankrupt the people in Ngami, and now this attack, convinces me that the people you are dealing with cannot be allowed to continue."

"Stopping them is not going to be easy. They will find a way to put me into the worst possible light the minute I become involved."

"It's an area so filled with uncertainties and apparent criminal intent that while it seems wiser to stay clear, if we do, then we are contributing directly to a broken system, in which blind power seekers will eventually engulf all of us. That is a big part of the reason I've decided to help you, to the best of my ability."

"Thanks Matthew."

"You will need to be present tonight, though."

"Won't help if they use it to finish me off."

"If you want the de Bruins to get financing, and you clearly do, you need to use video facilities to be present at the meeting with the financial people. No one in your organization would need to know about it. I'll try to keep you out of the direct negotiations.'

"I don't know what I would contribute."

"Even though the ore deposit is a genuine, tangible asset,the de Bruins, on their own, with one of them in a hospital, another hidden away in the center of Africa, and the older brother looking after their farm, are going to present a weak impression. They won't get the loan if you're not there. Financial organizations are set up to deal with solid businesses."

"You're probably right."

"I'm definitely right. So will you take part in the video conference?"

Michael agreed.

15

Ben was traumatized when Rebecca called him to tell him about the attack on Clare.

He had been driving to confront some miners who, apparently, were dissatisfied with with their supervisor. They suspected that the strike was a part of the ongoing, externally coordinated difficulties they faced, but they were not sure.

If not dealt with, the strike on its own could derail the project.

"Did they arrest the person who attacked her?" Ben asked Rebecca.

"They don't know who it was, but we do know that she called out 'Derek' as she was attacked."

Ben was silent for a moment then said quietly, "I think that was the name of the person she was supposed to meet in London when I asked her to go to Vancouver."

"What on earth would send someone after her from London?"

"I can't imagine. She'd just met him. Hell Rebecca, it's all just too much, I can't leave now or this place will fall in a heap. It's already half way there. And I can't just leave her there in hospital."

"Ben, I've just spoken to the hospital and to Clare. She is going to be okay. You need to focus on the business side of what's happening. Keeping the project going is critical. She would not want you to drop the ball now."

"What a mess," said Ben in an uncharacteristically soft tone.

"Is there any chance of you talking to the financiers?"

"No, the security people here would listen in. Can you arrange to record the meeting?"

"I don't think that's a good idea, Michael, for one, would not want it."

"I should get there myself, for Clare's sake if for nothing else," said Ben.

"There is nothing you can do here, time is slipping away Ben. It would take too long. She's safe in hospital."

"And when she's released?"

"It's the meeting tonight that we must concentrate on."

"I know Rebecca, but still...."

"You must keep going Ben. For Clare's sake as much as yours. I've asked Ed Chalmers to be at the meeting, he gives a very good impression and your rushing to Vancouver would not help. You can't even get to the meeting in time."

Ben hesitated trying to focus, "That is a good idea. He's quiet, cool, and knows what he's doing. He also knows the Ngami operation from the time he spent here last year," he said

"He's reading the information you sent now," said Rebecca. "And, one great thing is that what's happened to Clare has convinced Clement that he should help Michael Anders, and you. He's arranged for Michael to attend using video conferencing."

"I'm surprised about that. Michael has told me that he can't help."

"Michael's going to look incompetent if you fail."

"I suppose so."

That evening the financiers, and an American mining engineer, Paul Cartwright, met with Rebecca, Clement and Ed, to discuss the financial needs of the Ngami project.

Paul turned out to be an unusually tall man of about thirty-six years of age with broad shoulders and a trim waist.

"And he was an officer in the Green Berets," said one of the financiers as they introduced him.

Clement explained that Clare had been hurt and was in the hospital, but that Ed would present the facts of the financial case.

"Oh," commented Paul "what happened to her?"

"She was mugged," said Rebecca; and Clement added, before too much was said about the attack on Clare, "We'll also hear from the heir to the GVN Corporation."

"Vancouver is generally peaceful sort of a place, where did this happen?" asked Paul, not easily sidetracked.

"Stanley Park this morning,"

"I've heard of muggings there," said one of the financiers, "Is she okay?"

"The specialist is pleased with her progress."

"So to the financial case, you will also hear from the managing director of Ngami, who is also the heir to the GVN corporate empire," said the grey haired and statesmanlike Clement.

The video link was established, Michael was introduced and then Ed presented the financial and technical cases.

The financiers listened with interest and were clearly impressed.

Paul was not. He did not like what he heard about the mining method although Ed had managed to answer most of his questions.

"I still think that it sounds too idealistic," Paul said after Ed had handled his objections.

Michael said that the method used high technology to reduce the stress involved in underground mining, and to protect the environment, saying, "It's a beautiful and unspoiled area of Africa and safer mining has commercial as well as human advantages."

Paul answered, "Yes, Mr. Anders, I do see that the approach they're using would mean moving much less ground than with open-cut mining, but not more than traditional stoping. The difficulties that the machinery they are planning to use, can face, has been demonstrated on other sites in South Africa."

"They've been using the low-profile machinery in South Africa for at least ten years, and there've been improvements," said Michael. "They're at the next phase of the development of low-profile machinery in Botswana."

"Why is more money needed for machinery?"

"The summer has been very hot and it's slowing things."

"Slowing the machinery."

"That's right," said Michael.

"They're using room and pillar mining and LHDs."

"That's right."

"How are they breaking the ore?"

"That's fairly conventional for now."

"Ventilation is very important in those circumstances. Is it sufficient?"

"Yes."

"Who did the planning?" asked Paul.

"The people there."

"So Paul, we're expecting you to okay the technical aspects, and it sounds as though you won't be able do so?" said the older of the two bankers

"Not the way things stand."

"Could you not at least look at the project?" asked Michael, horrified at their closeness to failure.

Paul hesitated, "If I did look at the site it would still not guarantee my support and it would cost a great deal.

"We would need you to do that," said Michael.

"I'll have a closer look at what's happening," Paul said. "but, I'm as I've said, I'm not convinced that they're using a reliable method. In this shaky investment climate, their systems must achieve their targets."

"So what do you suggest?" asked Clement.

"A few days there and in South Africa would clarify the picture, one way or another."

Clement did not answer. Authorizing an investigation by Paul and the cost to the already financially strapped de Bruins were not something he could do.

There was a longish silence.

"Perhaps some interim arrangement?" asked Ed, looking at the older of the financial agents.

The woman nodded. Ed had impressed her. His quiet, slow, and deliberate diction, and manner, suited the Canadian approach to things.

Rebecca sighed with satisfaction at the value of Ed's contribution.

A short-term arrangement to provide extra funds to keep the Ngami operation running was then put in place. It was also agreed that Paul would leave for Botswana the next day and that they would meet again the following week, when he returned from the site.

After the meeting, the group had dinner in a restaurant with a rustic Canadian decor that included a Coastal Indian flavor. The view over the city completed its pleasant atmosphere and their table gave them a fairy tale view across Vancouver's twinkling lights.

Rebecca ordered a crab based entrée, with salmon cutlets, salad, and wild rice, for her main meal.

A Californian wine, chosen by Matthew Clement, went well with her choice and the meal was a memorable experience.

The excellent food, wine, and service meant that their outing was as pleasant as any Rebecca had experienced. She particularly enjoyed the company of Matthew Clement's wife, who she had not met before.

The Clements told the group that they often visited Vancouver so that Matthew, an avid angler, could fish.

Ed thought that their Bostonian accents matched their clear-cut points of view.

Paul enlivened the evening with his own fishing story, explaining that he sometimes fished on their ranch in South Dakota with explosives.

There was a shocked silence.

Paul mischievously continued, explaining that it was very efficient, and a lot quicker than using a rod, adding that if you froze the stunned fish, you only needed one trip each year.

"I suppose you hunt, too?" Rebecca said, to break the sudden, horrified silence, worried at what the answer might be from a Green Beret who fished with dynamite.

"With explosives?" asked one of the financiers.

"No, but I've a Winchester behind the seat of my pickup."

"Not something more efficient?" asked Clement.

Rebecca laughed and tried to get the conversation onto something less contentious. "And you were a Green Beret?"

Paul, on a roll, then told them several stories about Afghanistan that amazed them.

The group separated at about ten.

The financiers asked Paul for more details on why he thought the de Bruin's venture was impractical, after the two groups had parted.

"It is not entirely impractical, more idealistic, but it does seem well directed. My biggest problem is that in mining there's no room for gentle approaches. It's a tough business and always has been. I definitely need to see the operation to gauge their mixture of methods and how they are being managed," he said.

Paul was watching the cab, carrying the people representing the de Bruins, drive off, as they spoke, and thought he saw a car pull out behind them. Perhaps a coincidence, but it gave him a bad feeling. His training in counterterrorism had honed his sensitivity to danger, and he often trusted his instincts, at least to the point of carrying out extra checks.

His fears were well founded, Rebecca had become a target of the malevolent corporate conspiracy.

Paul wondered, as he drove back to town, what had really happened to the de Bruin woman who was supposed to have been at the meeting with them. He had not felt entirely comfortable with the way her absence had been so quickly passed off.

"Are you happy with what we've achieved?" Clement asked Rebecca as they drove away from the venue.

"Very. Ben's a bit like him. It might work out well," said Rebecca.

"Dinner surely wasn't boring. Was it?"

"What a character. I hope he likes what they tell him in Africa. I don't think he would pull punches."

When they got to the hotel, Clement asked Rebecca to see him in the morning to discuss her future and the South African situation.

"What do you have in mind?" she asked.

He avoided a direct answer by saying he needed to talk to the other partners in the firm before committing himself, and then changed the subject.

After they parted in the foyer of the hotel, Rebecca was left to her own thoughts about the future. She went to her room and phoned the hospital, to be told that Clare's progress was good. She emailed Ben about this news and used the message to explain what had happened at the dinner.

16

On the day after the dinner with the financiers, Matthew Clement made several calls to the leading members of his international firm about Binnett's South African problems. During these he realized that a quest to solve Michael's problems neither began nor ended with the the problems facing the dee Bruins and heir to GVN.

He found that there was a strong thread of concern running through the firm about similar trends in other theaters. He also found full agreement that Binnett's South African office needed to be checked.

This meant that Rebecca was his key to two puzzles; how to help Michael Anders, and, how to fix the South African division of Binnett.

When Clement spoke about this to Rebecca's branch head, Chris Bain, Bain told him that he was certain that Rebecca did not want to go back to Africa.

"Do you mind if I discuss the idea with her myself?"

"Not at all, Matthew. If you can get her to go, it will be good for the firm. The situation in the South African branch of the firm is really a worry, and tackling it without enough ground knowledge would be dangerous."

Clement then met Rebecca.

In the lounge facing out over the bay they exchanged greetings and found themselves a comfortable spot.

He told her about the help he needed from her to ensure Michael Anders' inheritance, the de Bruin's future, and the firm's base in South Africa.

"It's a very real need, Mr Clements, but I don't want to go to South Africa," she answered.

"We don't have anyone else who knows what's happening there. And as you well know we've been relying too heavily on Wilson."

Rebecca thought, "Poor you," but answered with a simple, "Oh."

"He's made the firm money alright, mainly from GVN, and he hasn't established anything that will operate, without them or with them. We need to build something more resilient, an alternate structure, and without your help I don't know how to get anywhere."

"I'm only an associate, and I don't know how to change things myself."

"You handle yourself well in all area in which you've been involved and you know more about what we face in South Africa than anyone else that I know of and you've asked to go to Botswana."

"A few days work to qualify the potential for Ben, is all I want to do there."

"We, the Ngami partners, and Michael need the same help, into the future, as much as the short term fix of the immediate problem."

"That might be, but I don't feel ready for that much responsibility," she said, thinking to herself, "Nor was I planning political suicide."

"I think you're a lot more ready than you believe," he answered.

"I would like to help, but I'd been planning to take a few days' break to think about my future. I've never dreamed of such a jump in responsibility."

"We'd like you to spend eighteen months there."

"You might be overestimating my ability," she said. "It's going to be a nearly impossible task."

"A well-paid one. If you take the job, your pay will match the responsibility. You could be paid there, in Australia, or here, depending on what we decide you want to do after South Africa."

"I'm not worried about money, but about failure. Can I think about it for a day or two and let you know what I want to do?"

"I have to do something quickly, so I'd like an answer by Saturday."

"Okay," said Rebecca, with equal degrees of relief and apprehension; at the immediate escape, and the tight deadline for her reply.

"To help you see our point of view, there's another thing I'd like you to think about. If you don't accept then I need someone else to run the South African operation. Is there anyone in the South African office that you've worked with that you think could handle the role?"

"I can't think of anyone at the moment."

"The other alternative is to get someone from somewhere else, and someone from the South African office who can support them. Is there a strong reliable candidate, who knows the territory, that you could recommend for either of the roles?"

"I'm not sure who I would recommend," she answered after a moment's thought. "But of course, I only spent a short time in the Johannesburg offices."

"At least you've met them. To me, and the rest of the firm, they're unknowns."

"I sure see the difficulty," she said awkwardly and made a move to leave, thanking him for the offer, and added, "Also, you should remember that it was me that GVN was annoyed about."

"Their reasons seem to have been confused, and they wanted you back the last we heard. Whoever takes over from Wilson is going to have to deal with that, no matter what we do."

"I think confused is too polite a term for that lot."

"It might be and it certainly needs attention."

"That's true, but I don't see myself as some kind of Joan of Arc. That office is not going to be easy to straighten out. I'm only an associate, not old enough and not experienced in running any sort of office. If I went into a situation that has such a high chance of failure it would be quixotic."

"I'm am slowly coming to a perspective that leads me to realize that people like Joan of Arc, or knights in shining armor are characters that are too often associated with the simplistic, feel-good stories."

"I see," answered Rebecca, not at all sure that she did.

"Sounds simplistic, I know, but if the world is left entirely in the hands of the totally opportunistic, then I think we might be headed for a new dark age in which society will slide into chaos."

"I hope that's not what we are facing," she said with an uncertain smile.

"Hopefully not, but what Michael and the de Bruins are facing are pretty calamitous situations."

When she got back to her room, Rebecca sat, for a while, and looked out on the snowcapped mountains. It was a beautiful day and she wondered what to do with the time she had been given to make up her mind.

Considering the assignment she thought that if she accepted the role being offered she would be busy enough to forget her loneliness, if that really was what was bothering her.

The work, they wanted her to do, would definitely help Binnett.

In human terms, because of the number of people involved in the dishonest manipulations, it would also be a measurably worthwhile effort.

In career terms the offer was a unique chance, an unbelievable opportunity for someone of her age.

She was, however, held back by several factors; she did not want to have to deal with either Wilson or Jack Anders at all, the stress of every day living, and the complexity that South Africa presented did not appeal to her at all. She needed someone to talk to, Karen back home in Australia was one option. Her pleasant, wealthy, and boring flatmate, was, however, not a good option, she seldom had any idea of anything more complex than her next holiday.

Then there was the impossibility of the assignment, she doubted the ability of the firm to deal with Wilson, whoever was given the direct responsibility for the exercise. He was a very well connected person and had few weaknesses that she knew of.

She started to phone Chris Bain, the Australian principal, then realized she would need to wait a few hours, to allow him time to get to the office.

Restlessly making herself a cup of tea she decided to take a drive inland, to Manning Park, another of the places where she and Ian Mui had had some great experiences. The three-hour drive from Vancouver would at least clear her head.

She packed, took the lift to the car park, and was soon on her way out of Vancouver on the Hope highway.

The Jack an van Zyl's agent followed her, asking on his mobile phone, as he drove off, if he should eliminate her on the road if the opportunity presented itself.

He was told to do so if it could be made to look like an accident.

Rebecca continued her attempts to adjust her objectives on the journey through the Cascade Mountains. She had never really planned an executive career. She, along with her childhood friends, had dreamed of having homes and families to take care of, to share her life, and fill her empty moments. She had, almost without thinking, gone from one seventy-hour week to the next. Promotion had followed on promotion.

Except in the case of Ian Mui, she had never had enough time to decide what her real ambitions were.

She accelerated, running the Mustang to its full ability, ignoring speed limits.

Exhilaration cleared her mind.

The agent following could barely keep up with her and, without the homing device he had attached to her car, he would have lost her.

She was relieved from the endless self-analysis by the beauty of Manning Park, and allowed her thoughts to be filled by the natural wonders surrounding her, slowing to better appreciate its wonder.

The gap between the vehicles decreased, but to the utter frustration of the professional killer Rebecca was already parked when he arrived.

He wandered across to reception and asked someone on the veranda if they had seen the drive of the mustang.

The cleaner told him that she had gone skiing.

He phoned van Zyl and told him where he was and that Rebecca had been going to fast to deal with on the journey from Vancouver, and was told to hold off in the resort area, unless he could organize a fall that would look accidental.

Van Zyl explained that anything that happened there would be very exposed.

Rebecca skied for a few hours, deciding, as the sun began to set, to phone her friend from the past, Ian Mui, in their Toronto office, to ask his advice.

They had kept in vague touch over the years, but had never recovered the magic of their time in Vancouver.

After he answered, they spoke for a few minutes about generalities and the latest company news.

She then told him of the opportunity she had been offered to restructure Binnett, and her doubts about accepting it.

Ian answered her by saying, "Rebecca, I can certainly see that you would be a very good choice. Considering your quandary, I think I would take the offer if I were you. Remember how we went over the aspects of career versus family and children before we parted?"

"I'm not sure that the path I chose was a good idea, though, Ian." She wanted to ask if he had married but told him, instead, that she had also called because she was in Vancouver and had been visiting some of their favorite haunts.

He answered that he avoided Vancouver with his family because her presence there was still too real to him.

When they had finished their conversation Rebecca felt like crying.

"His family!" she thought sadly. Another door closed. Another memory and nothing more. "I must get out of this mood," she told herself. The shadow of their lost time together had been pulling at her much as the child had in the Tea House. She bit back tears and then gave up and cried.

When she had regained her composure, she sat looking out of the window, unseeingly, for a while, before realizing that it was late enough to phone Australia.

She phoned and explained the offer to the head of the Australian office.

Her branch head, Chris, suggested she try to fit in with Clement's plans, adding, "You're certainly free to choose your own course, Rebecca. We need you here as much as ever, but if you don't go, he's also going to find it difficult to help either Michael Anders or Ben de Bruin, or the firm."

"Well, I've got till Saturday to decide," she said hurriedly.

He wished her luck with her decision.

Rebecca decided to go for a walk toward one of the spectacular trails.

This provided the agent following her an opportunity to kill her, but he held off because she never went far enough to be out of site of the resort.

17

When Paul arrived in Botswana it was hot.

Rebecca had told Ben that he would have no difficulty in picking Paul out as he was very tall. He saw Paul standing, looking uncomfortable, after the American had walked from the terminal building, wearing what looked like riding boots. But, as Ben later discovered, they were styled leather shoes, rather than high-heeled boots. Paul's size made it seem that he was artificially elevated.

Ben walked up to the South Dakotan and said, "Morning. You Paul Cartwright?"

"That's right, buddy, and you are Ben?"

"Yes, I am. How was the trip?"

"It's a long, long way. I stopped over and I slept, but I still feel completely dazed."

"Would you rather rest today?" Ben asked.

"No, I'm okay. Let's get to it, Ben. I know it's Sunday. If you'd rather not work?"

"The process plant runs around the clock, so we often have to work on weekends. Your exercise is by far the most important thing we have on at the moment, so don't worry about putting anyone out."

"Could we have breakfast before we start?"

"What would you like?"

"Whatever's possible."

"We can go to the hotel."

"Do I need to hire a car?"

"No. I've organized a company four-wheel drive. It's at the office."

"Great, thanks. I'll take a break this afternoon if that's okay."

Ben said it was, and they climbed into his vehicle.

"Hell, but it's hot," said Paul as they drove away in the air-conditioned comfort of Ben's vehicle.

"It's the worst I've ever known it."

As they drove on to the site through the undeveloped bush, that lay between the airport and the operations, five impala wander into their path.

Ben slowed as the animals stepped daintily along, and across the road, then he tapped his horn to set them into a graceful, leaping flight.

"I've certainly never seen anything like that near a mine," remarked the American.

"It's a well cared-for site."

They arrived at the hotel and went to the dining room, where they ordered their meals and sat drinking coffee while they waited.

"How's your sister, Ben? Have you heard?" asked Paul after they had been served

"She's out of hospital and improving."

"I've got a bad feeling about her that I can't explain."

Ben hesitated. He had remembered that Rebecca had said she had not told the financiers how Clare had been hurt. "Why are you worried?" he asked.

"Not sure, Ben. It's just a hunch, like a thought that won't go away."

"Did you meet her?"

"No, that's the odd thing about it."

"I was supposed to go to Canada myself. She should not have been there."

"You had to get finance, though."

"Yes, but she wouldn't have been there if I had gone."

"Rebecca has told me that you've had a tough time here."

Ben was filled with fear; for his sister, the venture and the future. He could barely think where to begin, what to say, or what not to say and tried to change the subject.

"Rebecca said you were a Green Beret in Afghanistan?" he asked. "Perhaps you have an extra sense about danger. Your hunches might be more precise than the average."

"Never thought about it much, but I think I sometimes sense danger. Not much we can do from here, though. Is Clare staying in Vancouver?"

"Yes. Once she recovers she'll need to be there until the finances are in place."

"Rebecca told me she was badly hurt."

"My brother is on his way there now."

"It's a very odd affair, I feel almost as though I'm back in the forces. There almost seems to be some lurking danger."

Ben thought, "Well you're definitely right about that," but said, "Green Berets work behind the line, the same as our SAS, don't they?" in a further attempt to get off the subject of the physical dangers they faced. He was worried enough about explaining the mining effort, and did not want financiers thinking their money was going to be put at risk.

Paul noticed the tension but continued, "Yes. They're what's needed in many situations today, where the threat does not come from large-scale invasion forces, but rather from small groups of terrorists who can't be fought with massed armies. The Green Berets and the SAS and similar forces in other countries, are small forces of highly-trained fighters. Even seemingly soft western democracies need them."

"Why are they called Green Berets?"

"It's a newish title, similar forces trace their roots back to Rogers's Rangers, who fought in the woods of New England during the French and Indian Wars in the eighteenth century. Confederate raiders were led by a guy called Mosby, who was also called the Gray Ghost because of his stealth and ability to elude capture."

"Why Green Berets then?"

"Green berets were issued to our Special Forces in Scotland during the Second World War. US Army Rangers and OSS operatives, who were trained by British Commandos."

"Commandos were what they called the Boer troops in the South African war?"

"That's right, but the people in Scotland were part of the British Army. A green beret was issued by them, to Rangers and OSS operatives who earned them. President Kennedy made the green beret into a part of the US Special Forces uniform, when they were preparing for a visit from him. The president sent word to the center's commander that all Special Forces soldiers should wear green berets as part of the event. He called the Green Beret 'a symbol of excellence, a badge of courage, a mark of distinction' in the fight for freedom. And many of Kennedy's sayings are sort of enshrined in our culture."

"Are SEALs Green Berets?"

"No. They're amphibious assault troops. Special Underwater Demolition Teams, Scouts, Raiders, and Naval Combat Demolition Units. They were sent in ahead of the main force to clear beaches and reconnoiter landing sites. These became today's US Navy SEALs."

"Pretty unique."

"Something to be proud of."

"And a Medal of Honor? Rebecca has told me." said Ben.

"I do have a few medals, but we were on the front line in the war on terror. Our missions were largely top secret. And while many are heroes, the honors they earn are usually awarded privately."

"And yours?"

"I'll tell you about it some other time. It's important, but not now. We've too much to do. I do think that you should check on your sister before we get going"

"Okay," said Ben and walked out onto the veranda to phoned the hospital in Vancouver. He was told that Clare had been released that morning, so he called the hotel, to be told she was out.

Finally he called her directly.

Ben did not talk about security or emails, he simply mentioned that Paul, the American engineer sent by the financiers, had a bad feeling about her safety.

"I'll be okay, Ben."

"Don't be so sure, don't take any chances."

"If you say so," she said. "I'll go back to the hotel and call you later so you know that I'm safe," she said, feeling foolish.

"Where are you?"

"Just going for a short walk along the foreshore, I've been inactive for days now."

"Clare, I think you should be careful, you shouldn't go where you are vulnerable. Where is Ed?"

"He's just left, I'm not far from the hotel. I'll go back now."

Ben returned to Paul after he finished the conversation and said, "That was uncanny Paul. She was walking around the waterfront."

"It's evening there now, isn't it?"

"Yes."

"Not a good place for someone to be walking in the evening when they're not well or injured."

"She's going back inside."

"Is she normally reckless?"

"She's very independent."

"I don't think it's my place to categorize her but she really needs to be careful."

"I've said so."

" Okay if we get down to work now?"

"We'll go to the planning office, and I'll show you what we're doing," said Ben.

After the call, Clare, thinking about Ben's concern, realized that he was right, she wondered at her own risk taking, and supposed that her overconfidence was a result of the painkillers she was taking.

She turned and walked back to the hotel.

When she changed direction, she noticed a man that she had seen earlier, a short distance behind her, changed direction to stay behind her, and felt a chill of fear. She walked briskly, her injuries slowing her, but was soon back in the hotel's foyer, feeling its warmth with relief.

She made her way to the coffee shop and then, turning, saw the same person, seemingly moving toward the elevators. Her heart froze and she moved out of his sight, trying to look casual.

She started to phone Ed and then remembered that he was away.

18

Ben asked Paul how long he was staying as they drove to the mine site after breakfast.

"Three days," answered Paul.

"You've come a long way for so short a mission. Have you got a lot on your plate back there?"

"That's about it, Ben. This is a sidetrack of sorts?"

"So you've nothing else to do in South Africa?"

"I need to check what you're doing with some people that I know in South Africa, in Rustenburg, on my way back. I don't have anything on for anyone else."

"So where would you like to start here?"

Do you have any equipment on surface?"

"I'll take you to the workshops."

They parked in front of the workshops and walked into the yard, where two loaders were standing.

Paul walked around the machines in silence and then said, "One fairly obvious point is that it looks too unwieldy to me."

"Too unwieldy?"

"You know, too big, too flat, the wheels are too small. How will all four wheels stay on the ground? The loaders must weigh a great deal and yet their torsional strength would surely be better with a more block like shape. It looks clumsy."

"I don't know. They've got to work in very low stope heights."

"Looks wrong to me."

"Peter Connor, our chief engineer, said something similar, but he's very conservative, likes machines that are foolproof."

"I would think about it, Ben. Foolproof is what's needed in mines."

"You are right of course and, since this setback, I've spoken to our mining engineers about increasing the use of traditional methods."

"Oh what was the result?"

"We have some scraper based workings, when the dip is severe, such as it is near the surface. These efforts could be increased, without much trouble."

"That's important."

"Your workshops are neat and spacious," said Paul as they walked back to the vehicle.

"Yes, the engineer in charge is good, he's worked in some of the best operations around."

"That's interesting, the same guy who does not like the looks of the loaders?"

"It is."

"So you can appreciate his advice?"

"Of course, but there are other factors."

Paul looked uncomfortable and nodded.

"What do you want to do now?" asked Ben.

"Can we see your plans?"

"I'll take you to the general offices to meet the mining people now, and you can hear what they think. Oh, and I should mention that Michael Anders is here, and would like to take part in our discussions."

"No problem. Is he the guy we spoke to during the conference call in Vancouver?"

"Yes, he's had more hands on mining experience than I have."

Michael, waiting to meet Paul, had been thinking about the visit to Southern Africa by Clement and Rebecca.

Rebecca was at that stage still in Manning Park, walking out of the Manning Park hotel, into the cool evening air.

She was followed by the agent as he asked, on his cell phone, how much risk he should take in completing the assignment kill her.

He was told to leave her, as she was not going to be involved in the refinancing of Ngami.

The longish walk tired Rebecca.

She had a sauna and then finished off the evening with a good meal, in the hotel's restaurant.

That night, in the warmth of her room, she read for a while, then decided to phone Dave Gabrielson, whom she had met in South Africa during her assignment there, and who had done some research for her, to ask his advice on what Matthew Clement had in mind.

The quiet and effective university professor had helped her find information about her grandfather's failed company during her difficult period in Botswana, the previous year. On that occasion he was almost the only person she had known who could step out of his world and understand hers.

Dave listened, to her, without interrupting, and, when she had finished her explanation, told her that he understood the difficulty of her choice, adding, "Rebecca, it's a major issue, the economic model the world is working within is not functioning at too many levels, and in too much of society. I and many others, perhaps more qualified than me, are not at all comfortable with the way we are slipping from one dissolute crisis to the other. In that context, GVN's efforts are worth addressing, as are Binnett's."

"A bit too much for me though."

"Perhaps not. Anyhow if you decide to take the role and need anything from me, I would help," he said, adding that whatever Clement wanted her to do, he would love to see her again.

After the conversation ended, she turned the lights out, fell asleep, to wake, an hour later, dreaming of the horror of her grandfather's failure. A disaster related to the same industry she was being asked to help, and which had, perhaps, also involved some of the same people.

She lay awake, thinking about what Dave had said, and decided that she had to return to Africa.

When Michael saw Ben and Paul arrive he walked out from the office block to meet them.

After introductions Michael said, "So, Paul, you say that you're familiar with mechanized mining?"

"There's not much else in the rest of the world, buddy."

"I mean with narrow seams, like we have with platinum," Michael replied awkwardly, wondering at the flippant reply.

"Of course I understand," Paul said and then explained that he had played a small part in implementing mechanized mining while with a machinery manufacturer in South Africa.

"Actual mechanized mining, or planning its application?" asked Ben, hoping there was not a problem with the level of the so-called expert's knowledge, and thinking that all he needed now was another false trail to deal with.

Paul looked at him oddly. "I worked for a consultancy that offered planning support to the industry. Mechanized mining in narrow seams was a popular new idea. There was one obvious drawback, and it remains a pitfall today. The lack of space is a very big problem. The low seams are claustrophobic and make working with the machinery, and work on the machinery, difficult. I'm not convinced that it's possible to use these machines in such narrow workings. In some places and to degrees, perhaps, but, in general, well, let's face it, narrow seam mining is very difficult. Years of experience and cheap labor have made the South African mines uniquely successful with mining narrow seams. And, their basic method of drilling, blasting, and shoveling rock into winch gullies, works, because there is so much cheap labor available. So all aspects of the method are well tried and tested. Greater mechanization has definite attractions, but I'm not sure it that it's economical."

"Let's look at the plans of what we're doing," answered Ben.

They spent some time looking at the mine plan while they waited for the mining manager to arrive.

"Who decides what should be done?" Paul asked the planning manager.

"We have engineers of our own, but we have to rely on the manufacturers to some extent."

"Wow, Ben, buddy, how can I recommend that?" asked Paul looking at Ben.

Ben was feeling progressively more put out by the bullying tone, something he'd sometimes experienced from people not fully familiar with what they were about. He said, "Paul, we're not experts. This is a new operation," he said, tensely.

"No one says otherwise, but you are asking for financial support and you have no guarantee from GVN, despite Michael's presence here," he said, looking questioningly at Michael.

Michael looked away.

"So my view is the decider and I don't approve work that is impractical," Paul continued, "and now, you're telling me that your plans are being helped along by machinery sales people? To be fair, I've come a long way to evaluate your operation. I can see the potential here, but mining is not a delicate science, guys. Decisions need to be made far in advance of the actual work. Machinery manufacturers sell machinery wherever and however they can. They are good for advice as long as you know what you are doing yourselves."

"I'm sorry, Paul," Ben said, feeling anything but. "I'm a geologist, not an engineer. Jeffery Nyasa, our mining engineer is more familiar with the details."

Paul asked where the toilets were and strode off with an air of dissatisfaction.

"Not too keen, is he?" said Michael, quietly to Ben, "I hope he likes what Jeffery has to say."

Jeffery arrived shortly after Paul's return. He had brought Anne, a robotics specialist, with him and introduced her to the American.

Paul continued his interrogation.

Jeffery was quick-witted and had a big sense of humor. He handled the tall, ex-rancher and ex-Green Beret's, abrupt way of finding out what was happening with ease. Paul was not the first tough customer he had met. Jeffery had grown up in mission schools in the then idyllic African country of Malawi. He had worked his way to his present position in the school of hard knocks, and the best colleges and universities.

Jeffrey was ably backed by Anne on robotic issues.

The pair clearly impressed the cynical Paul. "It seems that you've a good if not expert knowledge of mechanized breast mining," Paul said eventually.

"Expert? I don't know about that," replied Jeffery cautiously, wanting to quote the adage about experts being drips under pressure, but managing to maintain his diplomacy, "Anne is an expert, in robotics in mines," he said and waited a moment, resting on the planning table, before continuing, "We've used the experience people have had in South Africa, which of course means speaking to the manufacturers, who have international markets and contacts that we simply can't check on."

"Yes, I see. How many shifts are you working Jeffrey?"

"Two blasts per twenty-four hours; three stope faces, one to support, one to drill before blasting, and one to clean. Roof bolts are installed as face-side support, leaving an open area between the face and the first row of grout packs, of five to ten yards.

"The advance strike gully is carried between five and eight yards ahead of the panel face. Gully roof bolts are installed, after the roof bolt holes have been drilled with the gully rig, and then the face is drilled by the same rig. Where necessary, this unit also drills the down-dip sidewall. A large portion of the reef is blasted into the reef gully, and the balance is pushed into the gully by a remotely operated bulldozer. The rock in the gully, from both the face blast and the gully blast, is loaded and taken to the conveyor loading point by the loaders."

"Those large unwieldy-looking machines?"

"That's right, the ones that are overheating."

"What are your production targets?"

"We are aiming for twelve thousand tons a month per section, but we're not reaching them yet."

How much is it worth?"

"Underground milled head grade is four point nine grams per ton. Planned production is seventy two thousand reef tons per month, with six extra low profile sections. If we were to have an open cut operation, we would expect a head grade of about two point two four grams per metric ton."

"And the full production is worth?" asked Paul.

"About twenty-million dollars a month," replied Anne.

"Not bad."

"It all has to work. The robotic bulldozer is very effective in mirroring the work done by scrapers with more flexibility," she finished. "It's the loaders that are struggling."

"They've been a problem in low seam mining from the beginning," said Paul.

"Yes, but we've worked closely with the manufacturer here and they have assured us that the equipment we have is the latest."

"Look, you're probably doing the right thing, but it will be expensive, particularly until you get the operation running smoothly. I don't know what to say. The fact that you're having problems with the loaders overheating is a big negative guys, I've not heard of that issue anywhere else."

"It's the hot weather."

Paul looked at Jeffery and asked, "Is the ventilation adequate?"

"It is."

Paul looked worried, he sighed lightly and said, "Perhaps there is something more you can do? Can you show me the ventilation plans?"

"I'll get the ventilation engineer," said Jeffrey.

Ben's phone rang. He glanced at it and saw that it was Clare.

He said, "It's Clare," and moved outside.

"Ben, I was followed back into the hotel," Clare said.

"Where are you now?"

"I'm in the coffee shop. The person who followed me is here too. I'm frightened."

Ben did not know what to say or do.

"Perhaps phone the police?" he said inadequately.

"I'm not sure what the police would do, and we would end up with an inquiry we can't afford while we're looking for finance."

"What's the matter?" asked Paul, who had followed him outside.

"Just hold on for a minute please, Clare."

"Clare is in the coffee shop at the Westin Bayshore, frightened out of her mind. Someone followed her in from her walk."

"It's a very good hotel. She should be okay. Tell her I'll get someone there," said Paul and called an associate.

"Paul is getting someone to meet you, he'll be there in about," Ben said to Clare and looked at Paul to confirm the time.

"Fifteen minutes," said Paul.

Ben repeated the message.

"Thanks, Ben. I'm sorry to be such a nuisance."

"Clare you're in real danger, James will be there in a few days but until then you've got to keep out of harm's way."

"Okay."

"Phone whenever you like, and let me know as soon as Paul's friend has got you to safety."

After Ben finished the call, and before they were back in the office Paul said, "You know, I'm in an awkward position. This exercise clearly needs to be done at arm's length, but I sure can see that you're in an unbelievably bad situation as a result of the greed of these people."

"Thanks," Ben said.

"What's the matter," asked Michael when they got back into the office.

"Clare's worried, she's being followed."

"Is this danger related to your investment?" asked Paul.

Aware that they had tried to conceal the attack from the bankers, Ben hesitated.

Michael answered for Ben, "There have been some close shaves here. There are people who want to take control of this investment who are dangerous."

"Is that a fact?"

"Paul there's just so much at stake. It's a good investment. One that's really worth trying to take control of," Ben said.

"I sure see your point Buddy, I'm on your side here. You seem to be up against something very unpleasant, but when you're in an awkward position, it's an even worse idea to be using machinery that won't do the job. That's what I have a problem with. Let's look at the ventilation systems now," he said and continued his discussion with the ventilation engineer.

Once Paul thought he knew what was happening, he said that he wanted to work on his own for the rest of the day.

"What about tomorrow?" Ben asked.

Paul asked if he could carry out a final inspection, before heading for Rustenburg, where, he said, he had arranged to meet someone with whom he had worked; in the Platinum mining industry, on mechanized stoping.

Ben asked if he and Ann could attend the Rustenburg meeting.

Paul agreed.

The GVN heir then said that he had to leave as he was scheduled to attend an important Monday morning GVN board meeting.

Paul offered to take him to the airport.

On the way to the airport, Paul repeated that he had not seen anything that had changed his original concerns about the way the partners were planning to develop the mine.

Michael asked him if he should not perhaps consider the mine using a modification to what was being planned, rather than block the finance with a completely negative report.

"Michael, that would mean my doing the design for them, or them getting it redesigned, there's no short path to doing that. They don't know enough about what they are doing. The problem is that I need to assure the financiers that there will be a cash flow next week, next month, and next year."

"There is a split between traditional and the new method there now, they know what they're doing."

"Of course I've not had time to consider their whole approach and I will keep that in mind."

"Perhaps you could also estimate the value of their approach to the environment?" Michael asked.

"You only have to go into a low seam mine to understand why the people in them are sometimes desperate, Michael, but I'm an engineer, not a social scientist."

"So am I. And engineering things to be better is the way I like to work."

"Liking and financing are two different things, though," answered Paul.

They parted, both feeling discomforted, at the airport, and Paul continued on, to the hotel.

Michael was impressed with the picture Paul had formed, and he sent an email to Ben while he was waiting to fly out, suggesting he spend as much time showing Paul how flexible they were, as he did on explaining the advantages of mechanization.

After Michael and Paul had left, Clare phoned Ben to tell him Paul's associate had arrived at the hotel and had taken her to his home in West Vancouver, where she was comfortable and safe with the family.

"Could you have been followed?"

"David said not, and he seems very competent."

"That's great Clare, Paul is not happy with our approach but everyone here is doing their best. I think there is still a chance. I'll keep you posted," he finished.

"Thanks Ben. Good luck. I'll be thinking of you."

***

On Monday morning, Paul Cartwright met with Ben for breakfast.

They agreed that he would leave for Rustenburg, after he completed the day's planned inspection of the mine, and that Ben and Anne would travel with him.

19

The Monday of GVN corporate board meeting, in Johannesburg, began badly for Michael.

He set out early and was held up by two bad accidents. In one of these there was a pile of dead bodies next to a minibus that had been hit head on by a concrete mixer. The truck had crossed the median strip. The bodies had been thrown aside like so many sacks, to get the mass of traffic going.

This was, amazingly, less traumatic that the first accident which he had passed near his home. In this he saw a woman whose car he thought he recognized being pulled from the vehicle at a circle where a taxi had left via the wrong entrance for reasons he could not imagine.

Then, as he made his way into the meeting he almost walked into a director, who he had known most of his life.

She virtually ignored him.

Other incidents followed in short order, and Michael's fear that Jack was near to completely discrediting him became more of a certainty.

He gave up on socializing after being almost ignored by another director, who was renowned for her generous nature.

Having made his way to a seat at the corner of the boardroom table, near the whiteboard, he sat there gazing into the distance. Tall, lanky, and not as formally dressed as the average attendee, he looked out of place.

Jack's polished facade showed a touch of smugness as he watched his withdrawn-looking cousin. He was thinking how close he was to victory. His influence, in financial circles, and within GVN was extensive, and increasing; his efforts to conceal his true nature behind the polished veneer had succeeded, he had done a thorough job of discrediting Michael, without being obvious, and he was now an even better accepted member of the establishment than he had been before his cousin had arrived back from his overseas assignments.

Michael was not as withdrawn as he looked, he was thinking about a conversation he'd had that morning, with his new assistant Jane.

"Why are you looking so worried Mr Anders?" Jane had asked.

"I'm worried about this board meeting," he had answered, thinking as he did that he should not be saying as much.

"You must have dealt with many difficult situations before though, even when you got to Ngami with what you found wrong there?"

"I have, of course, many times and I hardly have to think about what I'm doing. Of course I always make sure I'm fully familiar with everything that's going on, before I confront anyone, if I possibly can."

"You've prepared for this morning though, judging by the amount of information I've found for you."

"I don't like board meetings."

"You haven't had much experience of them you?"

"No and not when I'm in a bit of a corner."

"your whole future is at stake, and you're dealing with masters in board-room politics."

He nodded.

"Perhaps when you get to the meeting you should picture yourself in a field environment rather than the sophisticated one you are going to find at the meeting."

"Perhaps."

"You've handled contention in the field, at a really bad time in Ngami."

"That's true."

"So your problem is the environment that they've created and are at home in. An artificial world that thrives on subtle put downs and innuendo."

"I think you're right but I'm still not sure about how to act or react," he answered.

"Your skill is results, you need to concentrate on achieving what you want, and ignore everything else."

***

Michael was not as withdrawn as his cousin assumed, he was ignoring the atmosphere, concentrating on the spreadsheet that he had prepared on his tablet computer, and thinking about awkward field meetings he'd managed, to his advantage.

After Jack called the meeting to order, he reviewed the previous meeting's minutes and then began a discussion of routine subjects.

His tone changed when he began describing a series of current crises the corporation was facing.

Michael was surprised at several of these. Among them a report that the platinum mines in Rustenburg were losing money.

He tried to question these statistics but was ignored.

He caught his breath, paused and then put his tablet down sharply causing an attention grabbing bang.

Jack was startled into a moment of silence.

"Jack, the industrial problems in Rustenburg are all over the press. If our mines there are not profitable, then I'd like some answers." Michael snapped.

"We've got a study team looking at the situation," Jack said dismissively a little less confident than before.

"When will you have answers?"

"Within the month," said Jack smoothly and went on to detail another difficulty, the corporation's interest in a major area in the Free State.

At one stage, it had produced as much as 35 percent of South Africa's gold. It was, he explained, in chaos. The mines in the region had become examples of decay. Centered on a garden city in the Free State, designed from scratch, with no traffic lights, only roundabouts, broad streets, and no high-rise buildings. Home to golf clubs, swimming pools, theaters, hospitals, parks, schools, and an airport, the development had at one time attracted people from all over with high salaries. It had six massive mines, with twenty-two deep level shafts, in which 122,000 people worked in 1994. Now it was virtually ruined by mismanagement and close to insane union demands. Mines were being plundered for scrap metal, and the farmers near the mines were struggling under stock theft and brutal farm attacks, tortures, and murders.

There was no discussion of GVN's involvement.

Michael's concerns about himself began to fade into the background as his concern about his inheritance increased.

Jack then turned his sights onto Michael himself, comparing Michael's efforts, and the Ngami project, to these disasters, turning to Wes Wilson, the South African head of Binnett consulting, for confirmation.

"Jack," said Michael before Wilson had a chance to answer, "that's right out of context."

Jack hesitated, again put off his stride, pushed his glasses toward his forehead, and looked condescendingly at Michael for a few moments. Then he turned again toward Wilson, clearly expecting some confirmation of what he had said.

Michael stood and walked to the whiteboard, saying, Let's look at a few facts, not giving Wilson enough time to become involved.

He had the full attention of the board.

Both Jack and Wilson hesitated.

"Let's look at Ngami," Michael said and started to write on the whiteboard, explaining the notes, clearly, and deliberately, as he wrote.

The list and its explanation showed that the actions that had led to the Ngami failure had occurred while Jack was directly responsible for the project.

Next to this he wrote a set of bullet points showing the actions he had taken to salvage the operation.

Jack had sunken back into his chair during Michael's delivery. He had not expected his younger cousin to be anywhere near as well prepared or to react so positively.

Michael concluded with, "There is too much confusion here, Jack. I'm organizing some studies of my own and would like to close the meeting now, to reconvene next week to review what I find. For one very specific point, why the hell have I not heard about so much of this before?"

There was a moment's silence.

Jack could not begin to explain anything to Michael without looking weak.

He nodded and closed the meeting.

Striding purposefully away, looking neither left nor right, Michael made his way up the fire escape, went to his office and phoned Clement, who had told him, on Saturday, that he and Rebecca were on their way to South Africa.

Clement answered immediately

After exchanging greetings, Michael asked, "When will you be able to start looking into our case?"

"We're on our way. What's the matter?"

"I've just left a board meeting in which Jack made a clear cut attempt to finish me, and on top of that, there are more problems with the corporation than I realized."

"So what's the situation now?"

"I've handled it, but I need a report from you on what is happening."

"I'm seeing our South African principal tomorrow."

"Great."

"With Rebecca."

"Perfect. One other thing is certain after this meeting."

"What's that?"

"Your firm's South African principal is definitely working hand in glove with Jack."

"He get's a lot of his work from GVN, but 'hand in glove?'"

"They were working together to make an idiot out of me at the meeting."

"Right Michael, leave it with me, I'll call you when I've seen him," replied Clement.

The story about the Free State mines at the board meeting had reminded Michael of something Rebecca Rosslynn had told him a few months earlier, after she had been withdrawn from the investigation of Ngami, about the failure of her grandfather's firm.

She and Michael had been sitting together on a flight from Ngami to Johannesburg, and he'd asked her where in South Africa she came from.

"Cape Town," she replied.

"Was your grandfather's firm in business?"

"He owned a small mining company. My father was killed in Angola. We lived with my grandparents."

"How did you end up in Australia if your family's business is here?"

"Was here."

"What happened?"

"Something like this business in Ngami. My grandfather lost everything he had in South Africa. We were residents of Australia by that time, because he was developing his interests there."

"Oh?"

"My grandfather's prospecting company discovered gold in the Orange Free State. He and the people in the town thought they were on their way to a tremendous success, but there was some problem with the geologists' activities that was contradictory. GVN was somehow involved in the subsequent development.

"Subsequent court actions found in favor of several famous and powerful personalities. The long and short of the tale is that my family lost everything."

"That would have been hard."

"We had to come back to South Africa, and the settlement of the company went on for several years, during which time we survived on charity. The second time for me, because my mother was destitute after my father's death."

Michael wondering at the similarities between Rebecca's family's bad experience and his own investigated her story using the GVN library and company records and found a clear link.

His assistant Jane came into the office at that moment and asked how the meeting had gone.

"Your advice was a big help. I put their influence and importance out of my mind and pictured a site meeting. It worked well. Thank you very much," he answered.

"So you got through okay?"

"Better than I could have dreamed, but there's a lot to do before the next meeting."

"What are you planning?"

"There are several problem areas that my cousin spoke of that I did not know about. The truth about what's been done in Ngami has been covered up by innuendo. I can't address all of it at once. I need help and there's no time."

So what's next?"

"I've asked Binnett's global managing partner who I've worked with in the States for help in researching the company's situation."

"Sounds good," she said, thinking that she would definitely ask him home to meet her father, who, although not in the league of the truly wealthy, was quietly successful. She thought they might both gain from the experience.

20

Ben thought Paul looked at ease on their flight to Oliver Tambo International airport near Johannesburg.

He was not as calm as he looked. Every aspect of what he had found seemed wrong.

Ben asked, "Are we at least getting somewhere in convincing you of the value of our efforts?"

"You are doing a great job, no doubt about it, and Jeffery, your mining engineer, is first class—he has clearly done his homework, as has Anne," he replied looking at her.

"They do a good job."

"I must still say that my problem is with low seam mechanized mining. It's simply not my idea of how you would get the best bang for your buck, especially in a spot as remote as Ngami. You yourself, are not really able to achieve the best results with your background in geology. Jeffery and Anne have had to learn about the approach from a distance. The one positive is that you're looking at increasing the amount of traditional mining, but its hardly a commitment. I think you need to emphasize you ability to swing to the less technical approach."

"Michael has helped, he's familiar with the GVN mines in Rustenburg."

"I'm not sure how familiar though Ben. You really need someone who comes from direct experience with the approach to do anything like this."

Ben nodded, and thinking about Michael's warning that he should emphasize the flexibility of their plans, said we can adjust what we're doing."

"It's the situation there now, that I have to comment on now, and then what you have planned in the short term," Paul continued.

Ben nodded and said, "There's something else worrying me. If you don't get back to Vancouver, the financing will be guaranteed to fall through, and with the ongoing violence in Rustenburg you could easily become another statistic during your visit."

"Surely if I'm not going to recommend the project they have no reason to kill me?"

"They don't know what you'll say."

Paul thought about Ben's advice and realized that he should consider it. Since he had not found enough reason to recommend the project, there was no need to continue the investigation.

Paul shook his head and sighed, "For now I don't think I should walk away."

Ben nodded.

They hired a car at the airport. Ben asked for the fastest one that the company had available and was given the keys to a German vehicle.

The choice was justified forty minutes later.

As they drove through the country after Marikana, between Pretoria and Rustenburg. A four-wheel drive came up quickly behind them.

Ben accelerated.

The four-wheel drive kept up, until the their speedometer indicated 130 kilometers per hour. The image of the vehicle behind them then began to shrink, and to disappear when they reached 150.

When they arrived in Rustenburg they decided to change cars and pulled onto a side road near the city.

No one followed.

After finding another hire company using a mapping program, Ben drove to the new destination using back streets.

He parked the first vehicle near the hire company and they continued the journey in a second high-performance vehicle, one that was suited for off-road use.

They had also decided that since their travel details seemed to have been exposed they needed to find somewhere different to stay. So they looked up accommodation using Ben's phone.

They chose the game lodge that the Ngami chief engineer, Peter Connor, who came from Rustenburg, had told them about.

Its advertising said that it was home to several species of antelope and other small game.

They figured a night at a game lodge would provide sufficient isolation to prevent their being surprised and booked three rooms using the web site.

The directions, on the web site, said to follow the N4 highway from Rustenburg toward Zeerust, a few kilometers over the Magaliesberg, a range of mountains. A location sufficiently close to Rustenburg for them to return to the next day's meeting.

Paul knew the Rustenburg area, having lived and worked there for two years during his previous time in South Africa.

The countryside lost its industrialized feel after they had crossed the mountains; after which it became a typical journey through native African bush, reminiscent of that found around Ngami. They arrived within an hour.

The game lodge owners, Andries and Mettie Nieweldt, welcomed them and explained that the establishment did not provide full board, but invited them to share their evening meal.

The three signed the register and were given their room keys. The lodge's owners suggested viewing the game at the river that evening.

They unpacked and Ben decided to take a rest.

Paul said he was going to see the game and Ann went with him.

A guide took them, with some of the other guests, to watch the wild animals coming to the river, in, what he told them, was a morning and evening ritual.

After absorbing the spectacle in silence, Paul turned to Anne and said, "African game is sure something special, isn't it?"

"I suppose when you live in the midst of so much of it, as we do in Ngami, you start to take it for granted."

"Hard to believe anything like this could ever be taken for granted," Paul replied.

"It's odd that we become used to things so easily isn't it?"

"Yes, humans are amazingly adaptive," replied Paul.

"But nature itself battles with industrial change like these areas have gone through," said Anne.

Paul, feeling unaccustomedly awkward, did not finish the conversation and went to take a shower before dinner.

"So you're American?" Andries asked Paul at dinner, after saying a formal grace in Afrikaans.

Paul tensed imperceptibly, expecting one of the sometimes annoying, sometimes tiresome, conversations one sometimes has in foreign places.

"Yes, I am. From South Dakota."

"Your history is a bit like ours."

"New Holland is a small town near where I come from, and of course New York was once New Amsterdam. We had no wars with the British as recently as yours, though."

"Yes," said Andries. "This farm was a battleground in the Boer War. Commandos operated from this very spot."

"I was a commando in Afghanistan."

"Bad situation that. It's hard to understand the Middle East. But a commando? That's something South Africans are proud of being. I was one, too. We did some amazing things."

Paul hesitated before answering. He did not want to talk about recent history. He knew that his long distant relatives, who had gone from Europe to South Africa, rather than America, deeply resented the Boer War. He decided that it would provide a safer subject for discussion.

"Your forebears gave the British a pretty good of a run for their money during the Boer war," he said.

"That we did. They won in the end, though, and they're still taking us for a ride."

"I suppose so, but the Boers took the land from the Africans before that."

"There were a few Matabele here, and a few Sotho, both of whom were invaders. This area has been invaded again and again. It's thought to be the cradle of life."

"The cradle of life?" asked Paul.

"That's right. In 1896, an Italian prospector found the entrance to a series of caves on a farm called Sterkfontein," said Mettie.

"Oh?"

"The caves are now regarded as one of the world's most important prehistoric sites. They found the oldest known skull of a humanoid there. It's called 'Mrs Pies'," she continued.

"How old?"

"About two million years," he answered.

"Holy cow. That is a bit historic. Where are these caves?"

"On the way from here to Krugersdorp, about thirty kilometers, I think."

"I've driven around there, but not heard of the caves before. Be worth seeing I guess?" said Paul.

"Probably. Many people think so. They're on the World Heritage List. They're formed by a series of chambers with passages between them. The biggest is about twenty-three meters high and ninety-one long, and there are many smaller chambers. There's a perfectly calm underground lake down there."

"Really?"

"Local tribes believe that the water has medicinal properties."

"So, did the prospector find the 'Mrs. Pies?'"

"Dr. Broom, from Pretoria did, in the 1930's I think. He made several discoveries of bones and other fossils among them he discovered 'Mrs. Pies', a well-preserved female skull of a species of early man. The skull is about two million years old."

"I've not seen the place, but I've always been traveling through, rather than exploring."

"This part of Africa must always have had a good climate," commented Ben, who knew the story and had visited the caves.

"There've been many other discoveries, and the museums of the world have dozens of other relics going back through thousands of years," the farmer commented.

Paul told Andries how the mine that Ben partially owned and operated in Ngami was looking at preserving the unique bushveld environment.

As that conversation progressed they discovered that Andries knew a lot about Ngami. He told them that he and his family owned substantial blocks of shares in both Ngami and other platinum ventures. "How is the mining going?" he asked Ben.

"Not to plan. Peter Connor gave us your son's name as someone to speak to about the effectiveness of mechanized mining," Ben said and then explained that, while the overall production record had just been broken, their new mining machinery was playing up.

"So what are you doing here?"

"Paul is an American consultant who's looking at the way we're mining the new deposit."

"The rumor mill says you're having trouble."

"We are bringing the new mine into production using some traditional narrow reef mining methods and moving toward extensive use of very low profile machines."

Andries asked them how much they knew about the use of mechanized mining by GVN's Rustenburg platinum company.

"We've been in touch with them throughout the development," said Anne.

"I suppose it's one of the reasons you've used the equipment," said Paul.

"My own feeling is that the people who produce the machines for GVN must make more money than the mine does," said Andries in an uncharacteristic interruption, it was an issue he felt strongly about.

"What makes you think that?" asked Ben,

"GVN's Rustenburg mines are in a poor financial position because of it."

"Our mine manager has spent time there and so has Anne, we have not heard much about about financial difficulties," said Ben.

"Jeffery and I did not really spend much time underground," said Anne.

"I've heard that they discourage visitors, and that they show those, who do get to go there, only what they want them to see," said Andries.

Ben, realizing that he had to redirect this train of conversation, asked, "Do many people in the district invest in the mines?"

"Yes, The platinum has provided good investment opportunities all through the second half of the twentieth century. Particularly since the invention of catalytic converters for treating exhaust gasses in cars.

"Farmers?"

"Farmers, a major tribe, who own a large part of one of the most successful platinum mining companies, and several others."

"A tribe? Are they still successful?"

"Definitely, and they're wealthy because of their holding."

"Why is it that they achieve more than the others?" asked Paul.

"The mining corporation that started the original mine with them is very competent."

"Do they use the latest low profile mining equipment?" asked Paul.

"No, not at all. They use, and always have used, the more traditional mining approaches."

"Seems to prove something?"

"Not about mechanization, they have a vested interest in keeping as many people in work as possible. Their equipment use, management, and interaction with their workers has always been good. They understand that there are many people in these parts who desperately need some cash and the pride that comes with having a job and the money, even though they are able to subsist on their tribal lands, they like to belong to something other than a place under a tree."

"Not unlike anyone else, I suppose," said Paul.

"So the fact that they have tribal lands enters into consideration."

"That's right."

The conversation returned to the problems with the environment that industrial progress had brought.

Andries said, "The present industrialization, which is choking once-beautiful places like Rustenburg, is really an extension of the flood of people that began arriving with the discovery of gold in the Transvaal Republic in the nineteenth century."

"When you look at what's been preserved in this beautiful reserve, it makes you realize about how much has been lost," said Paul.

"We gain and we lose with mining, but wealth creation is a part of mankind's heritage. We have tried to swing with the wishes of the Good Lord. My own son is a well respected executive in GVN."

"What a small world," thought Paul, and said, "You're right. Sustainable development is the catch phrase, but I suppose we don't see enough of it. The loss of the citrus orchards that were here is a pity, though."

"They're not really part of the environment, and many were pulled up because they were no longer profitable. It's a game, really. One step forward and two back. What we must do is replace this with going two forward and one back," said the erstwhile farmer.

"I remember the smell of the orange blossoms as one of the best features of Rustenburg," Paul said and then brought the conversation back to mining machinery. "What I need to know is whether there is any argument for using the latest mechanization techniques in Botswana."

"One of my sons has a senior position with GVN and they, with a British company, have been the main users of the equipment. While the price of platinum was increasing, the poor performance of the machinery was concealed by huge cash flows. Since the beginning of the global financial crisis, the main users of the equipment, who genuinely wanted to improve working conditions, has largely withdrawn from its use except in one area that has been very carefully redesigned to take account of known shortfalls in what they had done before."

"I'd like to know more about that effort," said Ben.

"I'll find out what I can and contact you tomorrow. Can you give me your cell phone number?"

As Paul prepared for bed after dinner, he wondered if anyone had developed a way in which a monetary value could be placed on achieving a best balance with people and nature. There was little doubt that the de Bruin's loss of their share of the project would mean a less caring effort to mine the valuable Ngami deposit. A negative report, from him, would almost certainly lead directly to the destruction of an environment that was at least as fragile as that in Rustenburg. But concluded that becoming a tree-hugging environmentalist would be unacceptable in his field.

21

Matthew Clement looked up at the new office block, while he waited for Rebecca. The aura of success, that the building displayed, was undoubtedly a measure of the difficulty he was facing in dealing with Binnett's South African principal. He was out of his comfort zone; in his decision to investigate Binnett, South Africa, in assisting the struggling heir to the GVN fortune, and in helping the de Bruins.

Rebecca's arrival lightened his mood. He liked the straightforward Australian associate, and felt pleased that she had agreed to help him.

"Long flight?" he said, after greeting her.

"Too long, but I don't feel too bad. I stopped over in Singapore."

"Great place, isn't it?"

"Sure is. I'm always promising myself that I'll stay there for a longer period than a stopover. I love Little India, the smell of spices and the food, the variety of goods for sale, and the people. It reminds me of the times I spent as a child in the Indian markets in Durban. They were like an Aladdin's cave to me."

"Yes, I like it, too," said Clement. "Though my favorite place there is the Botanic Gardens."

"They are good, aren't they?"

"Really interesting. The orchids are exceptional."

"Singapore exports orchids, don't they?"

"Yes, in big quantities."

"And the food there. They have such a variety of cuisines."

"They sure do. It's hard to decide where to eat. The Indian buffet in Raffles is very good."

"That's the old colonial hotel there?"

"Yes, its got a special feel to it."

"My favorite food is chili crab. I buy it down by the river. It's the best I've ever tasted," said Rebecca.

"So, to Mr. Wilson. Could you give me a few minutes on my own with him, and then join us?"

"Of course."

"I'll call you after I get an idea of where he stands and what his attitude is. Would about twenty minutes be okay?"

"That would be fine Mr. Clement," said Rebecca.

Wes Wilson greeted Clement with a warm handshake and a large beaming smile. "Well, Matthew, this is an unexpected honor, how can I help you?"

"As I told you on the phone, we're going to conduct a management audit of your operation."

"That's the first we've had of those. Our results are so good."

"They are, but we have to do this to ensure our standards are held, even in this successful environment."

"We? Who have you brought with you?"

"Rebecca Rosslynn."

"That's a surprise."

"She's very well thought of."

"Oh?" said Wilson skeptically. "Would you like tea or coffee?"

"Coffee would be great, thanks."

Apart from the cup of coffee, Clement was not given any further feeling of cooperation or welcome.

He was shown a comfortable chair while Wilson 'finished something off.'

When Rebecca arrived, after receiving Clement's call, she found Wilson sitting behind his mahogany desk.

The office was as comfortable and expansive as she remembered, and Wilson looked to her like a self-satisfied dictator.

Clement was sitting awkwardly at the coffee table away from the desk, near the window. His face showing discomfort, something she had never seen before. He held a newspaper. A half-finished cup of coffee stood, looking neglected, on the table next to him.

"Back with the principal this time, Rebecca? I thought we'd seen the last of you," said Wilson.

Rebecca didn't answer.

He came out from behind the desk. "Please make yourself at home," he said, gesturing to a chair near Clement and then ambled across to join them. "Tea or coffee, Rebecca?" he asked.

"I've just finished a coffee downstairs, thanks."

After a moment or two of silence, Wilson said, "Now that Rebecca is here, can you tell me what you have in mind Matthew?"

"There are a few aspects of Binnett's South African business that I want to check," said Clement and sat forward in the chair, looking more like his usual self.

"We have a better return than any division in the world," said Wilson, without losing his smirk.

He was sitting upright in the lounge type chair, rather than back, so that he overlooked the other two.

"I've had a major complaint that I want to check, and I can't do it on my own, so Rebecca will be helping me."

Wilson's smirk faded slightly.

"You've got all my reports?"

"I want Rebecca to look at what's happening," Clement said. "I'm using her because I don't have enough knowledge of the area. So I'll work in parallel with her. She'll do the legwork, and I'll stay in the background."

"It's going to be very difficult for me. How will I be able to explain Rebecca looking at our operations?"

"That's perhaps true, but all companies have audits of one form or another. That's what this is."

"To be fair, she was not the greatest success when she was last here."

"You find a problem with her ability?"

"No, but—"

"Wes," Clement interrupted, "I've had a complaint from a major client in an international firm, and I need someone who is familiar with South Africa to help me look at what's happening here."

"That can only be from GVN, and the only one there who is likely to complain is Michael Anders."

"He's entitled to do so, isn't he?"

Clement was worried, conscious of the fact that Michael, and the de Bruins, were up against something outside his experience, in Wilson. Especially since Wilson was working with the apparently equally polished Jack

Anders. There was so much at stake. He did not know enough about where the firm stood in the South African market. He was responsible for the business and could not afford to lose South African customers. Although opportunities in South Africa were better than in most of the world, he had no idea where to pick up on those that existed or where to begin developing other customers. Now by having had Michael drawn into the conversation at such an early stage, he was on the wrong foot.

He said to Wilson, "He is taking over the GVN corporation."

"For us it's a question of who pays the bill. The managing director approves expenditure, and Jack Anders is the managing director."

"Acting managing director. The company is Michael's inheritance."

"I haven't heard from him."

"He has bypassed you, because he's not happy with your efforts. The reason in not only that I know him personally, he's not happy with your work, and feels threatened by it. So some questions arise on what you're doing."

"That's not the situation."

"I need to check," said Clement, "and I need your cooperation. I'll be working with Rebecca on preparing an independent assessment."

"And Rebecca is independent?"

"From your operation."

"I consider it to be very likely that she will be biased."

"Look, Wes, if you could just provide her with what she needs, we'll get moving. We can discuss anything you don't like about what she says or does, when or if problems arise."

"So you're not happy with my reporting?

"No. I'm not happy. Michael Anders has asked me to look into what's happening here. That's why I'm here."

"Michael Anders is slipping, I believe," said Wilson, moving the conversation out of Clement's field of knowledge.

"I've known him for some time and don't think he is the slipping type. He's no extrovert, but I don't think he's weak. Anyhow, what I want is a general review of what's happening here. You have other clients, don't you?"

"Things change, people change, and the world is changing. We don't have that many clients other than GVN at the moment."

"All your eggs in the one basket?" asked Clement.

"You could say that, perhaps."

"Not a good way to run a firm like this, though, and, Michael, the heir, is not happy with our work?"

"Michael is in a bad position, of his own making. Whether that's because he's weak or anything else, I don't know. I don't have much to do with him, so I don't know what his agenda is. Michael has made some bad mistakes.

Take Ngami for instance," he said, looking malevolently across at Rebecca.

"That's a good point. I'd like to know a bit more about what happened there. For instance, what was wrong with the work Rebecca was doing?"

"That's water under the bridge. Why worry about it now?"

"You brought it up. It's a valid point. It was an odd exercise. We are a firm with a good reputation and need to keep that reputation. Our name is as old as any in the business and very well trusted. Ngami nearly destroyed Rebecca's reputation, and that reflects on Binnett."

Wilson's smirk had gone, replaced by a more intense look. "I thought we were about making money, and I do that rather well. Even though it seems to be unimportant to you."

"Wes, I am absolutely concerned about making money. However, if we were making it by selling illegal substances, I would not want to be involved, and it would be my duty to find out why we we're off track. People have certain inalienable rights and should be able to have them respected by firms of our size and caliber, and I'm not alone in that belief."

"You might be in a minority, though, Matthew."

Matthew Clement shook his head irritably, "That's not the point and you're right when you say things change. That's why I'm here—to make sure we're happy about what is changing. We need to take stock of what we're doing. That's my role. As a firm we believe that there is a tomorrow, and that we need to look after it. So now I'd like you to arrange for us to talk to Jack Anders."

"Fine," Wilson replied and contacted Anders while they waited. He arranged for a meeting the next morning, then stood, and asked if they could excuse him, as he had other urgent business.

Clement and Rebecca followed him out of his office.

"That was a bit difficult," said Rebecca, once they were in the coffee shop downstairs.

"I knew it would be."

Rebecca remained silent. Her bad feeling about the role she was to play was becoming intense. She was certain that money was the basis of business, and it was becoming steadily more certain, to her, that their shaking the GVN money tree might be a disaster. "Interfering with the GVN Binnett relationship might cut the firms income too severely," she thought, but said nothing.

No matter who the good guys were, without cash flow there would be no firm.

"Shall we have lunch?" suggested Clement.

"That's a good idea, and perhaps a glass of wine?"

Rebecca and Matthew Clement spent an uneventful afternoon shopping in Sandton.

"You're very quiet, Rebecca," Clement said, toward the end of the day, while they were enjoying scones and tea, in the annex to a pleasant gardening shop.

"I'm worried," said Rebecca. "Wilson is not going to walk away from his role."

"He's certainly entrenched, and we don't have much leverage. We'll have to see what Jack's attitude is when we see him tomorrow, but I'm not too hopeful. Whatever happens, we need to detail the work Binnett has with GVN quickly and accurately."

"Yes, it doesn't look as though we'll get much cooperation," she said.

"It's certainly going to be difficult. The statistics Wilson provides in his reports are good. We can audit Binnett's actual exposure to GVN, but Wilson's competence can't be questioned until we can come up with something specific."

22

After a good night's rest, at the game lodge near Rustenburg, Paul took a walk down to the river with one of the lodge's rangers, and was treated to a repeat of the evening's parade of game, in the early light.

His thoughts drifted again to the horrific changes that mining had wrought in this part of South Africa. The forty to sixty years, that it had taken to completely trash Rustenburg, did not imply much of a future for the world. Not his problem he supposed or tried to convince himself.

Andries appeared while they were loading their vehicle before leaving.

They thanked him for his hospitality.

He wished them well, and said that he would find out all that he could about mechanized mining from his son.

Laurens Bredenkamp, Paul's ex-colleague, met the three in the foyer of a pleasant venue near Rustenburg Kloof. The hotel's luxurious decor made Ben feel out of place.

"Nice place," said Paul, thinking that many such aspects of South Africa were in a class of their own, and wondered, not for the first time, at the ongoing extreme differences in the lifestyles of the ruling classes, and those of the disenchanted platinum mine workers.

Laurens exchanged greetings with Paul, as old colleagues do, spending a few moments catching up on their experiences.

***

The group's location, in Rustenburg, was noticed and reported to van Zyl, by people his agents knew, shortly after the group's arrival at the hotel.

Van Zyl and Jack Anders discussed their options and decided that Rustenburg was violent enough for an attack on Paul to be taken as part of the district tension, and instructions were issued to get rid of him.

***

In the hotel, Laurens led the group from Ngami to a small, plush conference room where he introduced them to the machinery supplier's people.

"Have you arranged the visit, to the mine that you planned?" asked Paul.

""It hasn't been possible, they're too busy at the moment."

While they were making themselves comfortable, he showed them a series of slides on his experience, explaining that he had last worked for the company, that pioneered the use of narrow reef mining machinery, several years earlier, in 2007, and that he had taken up his current position with mining consultants when that company had, at that time, scaled down their mechanized mining efforts.

One of the company representatives then summarized their experience, and explained how their equipment was used.

Paul asked a few questions.

Ben had realized that both representatives were salespeople rather than technicians or engineers and was furious. He had specifically asked the company to provide technical experts.

Seeing Paul's look of disappointment at the level of experience, Laurens said, "You know that the methodology has had to be continuously adjusted?"

"Yes, and you've not been directly involved in the last few years?"

"No."

"I do need to speak to someone who is up-to-date or visit an operation," said Paul.

"Unfortunately, I haven't been able to organize anyone, and, now it seems, the people in Ngami have sent us marketing specialists."

"I specifically asked for technicians," said Ben.

"We are technical," said one of the machinery representative, a rather attractive blonde woman.

"Makes my work more difficult," said Paul, glancing at Ben, who shook his head and looked embarrassed.

Ben had not told the suppliers that he was going to be in Rustenburg himself and clenched his teeth wishing he could get hold of the 'upper class accented' machinery manager that he had spoken to the previous day. So very much hung from Paul's decision and what the American was being fed now would simply confirm Paul's view; that the Ngami design was little better than an extension of the machinery company's marketing plan.

"Let me explain the background anyway, Paul," Laurens said.

"That would be good," thinking that he did not need to hear anything about background.

Laurens began by saying, "There have been changes in machinery use in narrow seam mining over many years.

Driven by safety and by economics. Huge improvements have been made. As you know, underground mining is very complex and dangerous. It involves everything from rock mechanics to electronics and, of course, each of these factors is affected by cost."

"To an outsider the huge number of people involved seems to imply no technology at all," said Paul.

"The technology is extensive, and people are important, but there are large numbers of people because of the huge scale of the operations."

"Not too much is covered in the press, despite the recent reporting of unrest in the unions."

"You won't find too many people rushing around saying this is good or that is bad in this industry unless it's at least partially true. You also probably realize that industrial unrest is not always justified. Certainly there is something wrong now, but it's political as well as industrial, and very difficult to deal with, so I won't go into that, if you don't mind."

"Good. I should mention that I know a lot more about mining in open cuts, and underground mining that can be done by large machines. My experience of narrow seam operations is limited to the two years that I spent here as a consultant," said Paul. "Underground mining, in narrow stopes, with the only break in the pitch darkness, coming from the flicker of cap lamps, is definitely a claustrophobic experience."

"At the face, drills clatter like the hammers of hell and water mists the air. Stygian blackness alternating with the semi light. Underground is not my favorite place."

Laurens nodded "Underground mining takes some getting used to," he said, and continued, "but it was worse in earlier ages. For centuries people have drilled holes using hammers and chisels."

"With no water the dust was terrible and the miners only had a life expectancy of thirty years or so, before they died an agonizing death from solidifying lungs," commented Anne.

Paul shook his head and looked down.

Laurens continued, "Explosives were then used to break the rock. The introduction of pneumatic rock drills in the early twentieth century was a big advance on this. Smaller, lighter, handheld units, that were easier to use, followed. The arrival of air legs then allowed a miner to apply increased pressure to the drill and this increased its capability. These were followed by water-powered rock drills, which were introduced in the 1980s," said Laurens using illustrations.

"Were they better?"

"They have twice the power of pneumatic rock drills and are nowhere near as noisy. So yes, they are in some ways better."

"Why are pneumatic drills still used?"

"There are a number of reasons," said Laurens. "One is that, although high pressure water is available, it still has to be disposed of if it's used to power a drill. So it has to be pumped out of the mine, and the apparent energy saving is not quite as big as it would at first seem. Pressurized air is also easier to handle than pressurized water, and in platinum mining, there is a problem with processing the ore once it has too much water mixed with it."

Anne joined the discussion again, by saying that she had experienced the complexity of this world when. as a junior engineer, she had spent a semester in a rock drill repair shop, running it while the person in charge went away. She said, "It's a very complex production line and any slip in repair quality shows up as an inefficiency, which immediately affects production bonuses. The miner's bonuses depend on the efficiency of the drills, so if there's any problem with a drill the miner complains immediately."

"So they complain immediately?'

"Yes, and usually with a high degree of annoyance."

"Good experience?"

"It was one of the most interesting things I have ever done, a given mine uses so many that a huge effort is involved in their repair and maintenance. Literally hundreds have to be ready, to perform to a standard acceptable to someone whose income depends on the individual drill."

"Must involve quite a few technicians?" said Paul.

"It does and gave me an idea of the complexity of running and repairing machinery that's used in such a huge scale of high production. More equipment needs more complex backup," Anne said.

"That's why we have such a good workshop system at Ngami for the mining machinery," said Ben.

"I noticed how professional the workshops were," said Paul "So you're well equipped to look after the advanced machinery."

"That's a big plus," said Laurens.

"What about scraper winches?" Paul then asked. "When did they arrive on the scene?"

"Scraper winches began to replace gravity and shovels to move rock—both in the face and the gullies—in the 1920's," said Laurens.

"Hell of a long time ago, and they still use them in most narrow seam mines."

"There are large numbers of them in use and moving them and repairing them is a huge task," commented Anne.

"So, Paul, your question is why anyone would replace the commonly used scraper systems with trackless vehicles?"

"That's about it. In narrow seams, scraper winches work well."

"And the back-up logistics are in place, understood, and work," said Anne. "The same is true in the use of loaders used in the development of tunnels."

"Why has no attempt been made to use them in stopes?" asked Paul.

"There have been experiments in their use but the space is so low. In the development of a tunnel there is more headroom, the loaders don't transport the rock more than a few paces. They lift product up and over the loader into a rail car behind the loader. Compressed air driven, in that environment, they can load much faster than people shoveling. And they're robust. There is also an existing set of knowledge and experience about their repair and operation," answered Laurens.

"They're no good in the mine stopes stopes because they are lower in height than a dining room table. There is no room to lift rock over the loader, it has to be shoveled off the ground and then carried by the loader. Transporting the ore, in awkward roof heights, is thus added to the time and work requirements of loading," said Anne. "Imagine trying to drive a large load of rock around under a vastly extended dining room table."

"I can't imagine it being practical at all," said Paul. "When and why did the low profile trackless equipment get into the picture?"

"The first four low profile face drilling rigs, for use in the chrome mines, were delivered to South Africa in early

1999. By the end of 1999, the productivity of the rig had been demonstrated and additional units were on order."

"That's chrome mining—what about platinum?"

"The reef is narrower, and because of that, the problems are worse."

"It was tried though?"

"The population was more stable at the end of 2000, labour was harder to recruit than now."

"Not so many refugees?"

"That and other factors. Mechanization in the platinum mines was affected by several 'environmental' factors. Around the beginning of this century it was becoming more difficult to recruit handheld rock drill operators. The job involves hard physical effort and has lost the 'leading' status that it once held. AIDS was also an issue, with half the workforce being infected. When you feel sick, work suffers. Noise increases occupational health costs, and it is dangerous."

"So platinum mining was handled separately."

"Completely, because the reef is so much narrower. The platinum mines picked up on the low profile equipment developed for the chrome mines. The chrome ore body has a width twice that of the platinum reef."

"Mining more waste rock than you need is of course impractical. Every extra scrap of rock mined along with the reef is exactly what it is called, waste. Allowing extra height, than the reef width, results in less platinum per unit of rock extracted at the shaft head, and thus lower precious metal percentages."

"Were the advantages achieved?"

"Not really, for one thing, mechanization is a big change from conventional mining at all levels of organization, from operators to senior management."

"And?"

"Management becomes a problem. Every part of the backup system must work, one inefficient machine is far more of a problem than one inefficient single drill as Anne was explaining."

"Bigger output, bigger problem"

"That's right, then there were many teething problems in the designs. The face drill worked well; the roof-bolting machine was also good enough, but the loader was unsuccessful. The traction drives were problematic and tire consumption was almost unmanageable."

"So how did they keep going?"

"A dozer was introduced and it improved loading. They changed the arrangement of the excavation from board and pillar to what's called mechanized breast mining. Improvements were also made to the loader design. They improved the tyres and many other problems were addressed,"

"Yet after getting the method working, they stopped most efforts during the global financial crisis, didn't they?" asked Paul.

"Conventional mining provides the required output, on time, eighty-five percent of the time and very low profile machinery was not getting close."

"That answers my question," said Paul, looking at Ben, and then he said, "So the required result was not achieved?"

"Nowhere near. Initial calculations suggested that, with a fleet of one face drill, one roof-bolting machine, and two loaders, it would be possible to achieve a production rate of sixteen thousand tons per month."

"Not achieved?"

"Not even close. Following the initial work, it was recommended that the production target for a suite of equipment should be ten thousand tons per month."

"What target was achieved?"

"The target was finally reduced to six thousand five hundred tons and not achieved."

"So the system was unsuccessful?"

"That's right and the loader was the biggest problem by far, and the next was the malfunctioning backup systems."

"And you're having trouble with the loader," Paul said to Ben.

"Our's is the latest development."

"We didn't have problems with overheating, but traction was a disaster. They used a novel drive—a fully hydraulic powering system with hydraulic wheel motors.

Tyres failed at a huge rate. Chains were tried. They could not be kept tight. The wheels were too small. They tried a redeveloped tire that gave a better life and traction but it wasn't good enough."

"So they gave up?" said Paul.

"As I've said, the method, the machines, and their application all had problems and the company decided to move away from mechanized mining in 2008," answered Laurens.

Ben, feeling desperate, said, "But that's not the last word."

"That's true. A single, well-organized project was set up, and it's working better, but you need to speak to someone who is more familiar with their results."

"GVN has not moved away from the approach?"

"I don't know their story, Paul."

"They are still using the method Laurens has described," one of the representatives answered.

"Were their problems as bad?" said Paul.

"They work around the limitations."

"How?"

"They use a lot of equipment."

"What about cost?"

"They accept that they have to pay for the benefits."

"Are all their operations using it?"

"They are a much smaller company where platinum is concerned. They have two mines, and the method is extensively used in both of them," answered the representative.

Paul felt they had covered as much as was possible, and that there was no good argument for using the machines, so he decided to end the meeting.

He declined an offer of lunch, saying he wanted to rest before the long flight back to Canada. He thanked Laurens for the information he had been given and they agreed to meet up when next Paul was in South Africa.

Laurens and the two representatives then left the venue together.

"So Paul?" asked Ben as the three walked from the conference room.

"Ben, their targets were lower than yours and they never achieved any of them."

Ben did not answer and looked ahead, decidedly unhappy. "What if we change now to the traditional method?" he asked.

"Completely restructure everything you've done and waste the capital. That's going to be too expensive now. I can't go back there and say you've changed your minds completely."

"No, I suppose not."

Anne wishing she was somewhere else said, "Paul are you going to follow up on the single project they spoke about?" she asked.

"I really am tired and the method is experimental. I can't recommend something with such high risks."

"Do you mind if I contact Andries about meeting his son?" asked Ben.

Paul frowned, and then said he would wait for the reply.

23

In Johannesburg the atmosphere in the Binnett building was decidedly chilly. Wilson was confident, in control, and barely cooperative.

Matthew Clement was becoming more worried by the minute, his uncertainty was reflected in his uncharacteristic awkwardness.

Rebecca hid her doubts as she and Clement headed for the GVN offices, to attend the planned discussion with Jack Anders. They had arranged to meet Wilson at the venue and he was waiting for them in the foyer.

Jack arrived shortly after them, smiled pleasantly at Wilson, shook his hand, then turned to Clement, with a marked change in posture, his attitude almost threatening.

"Nice to meet you, Matthew," said Jack in a tone that conveyed no more warmth than did his bearing.

"Likewise," answered Clement. "Your firm is a very important client of ours."

Jack nodded vaguely to Rebecca.

"I've arranged somewhere we can talk," said Jack, and turned, to lead them across the immaculate slate floor, down a passageway, to a conference room.

To Rebecca the room felt archaic, out of place in the otherwise well-fitted building. It was badly lighted and hot.

Jack made no attempt to adjust either air-conditioning or lighting.

After closing the door behind him, he sat down, opposite the three Binnett people, appearing restless, giving every indication that he did not have much time to spare, and then said, "Wes tells me you are reviewing your South African interests and that you need my help."

"We need to look at the documentation, terms of references, and progress reports for the work we're doing for you."

"Why?"

"To ensure our standards are being met."

"Why are you talking to me in particular?"

"Because you represent GVN."

"I'm perfectly happy with your firm's performance in South Africa, and in particular with Wes's contribution, so we have no interest in checking on his efforts."

"I see," said Clement, "we do, however, need to review our operations in South Africa."

"We have a great deal of sensitive work and I don't want anyone, that we don't know, or are worried about, interfering," answered Jack.

"Surely you're not saying that you object to us reviewing our firm's internal arrangements?"

"Of course not, but I am saying that your firm is not the only one in town. If I find you're creating problems for us, I'll start canceling work," he said, then looked at Rebecca and continued, "Ms. Rosslynn was not particularly successful when she was here last year. Where in your firm would she be used, in relation to your many GVN orders?"

Rebecca looked unhappy, while she had been pessimistic, she had not expected anywhere near this level of attack.

Clement hesitated before answering. "We haven't set up our work plans yet. We wanted to get your opinion before formalizing what we're doing."

"My opinion is that nothing your firm is doing for us needs checking, so we don't need any of the work you seem to be talking about, but I'll help where I can. Please let me see the outline of what you want to do," he said.

"As I said we wanted this to be an informal discussion and will formalize the schedule based on what you would like us to do."

"I have no issues with Binnett's work with us."

"We'll prepare a schedule of what we want to see ourselves and bring it back tomorrow."

"See you tomorrow then."

"Thanks."

"After lunch at say two?" said Jack.

They agreed.

Striding back to his office, Jack thought irritably about his background, his life, and his closeness to victory. If Clement thought he was going to affect his plans, he was in for an unpleasant surprise.

His thoughts then turned to his cousin, Michael, whose taking over the meeting on Monday had been a shock. The interrupted board meeting, when it resumed, was going to be critical to both their lives. Until then he had to keep Clement clear of anything remotely contentious. He wondered if he should arrange to have the pair stopped by some more effective means and phoned van Zyl to tell him to get rid of Clement in an accident.

Clement, Rebecca and Wilson stopped for a moment in the foyer of the GVN building after the meeting.

"What now?" asked Rebecca.

"Back to our offices, to start the review," said Clement.

"Do you have any idea where you would like to start?" Wilson asked once they were there.

"We need a list of work you have in hand, and details of problem areas that you have worked on in GVN," Rebecca said, "We most particularly need to review the Ngami project."

"It's stored in the archives."

"Are they difficult to access?"

"Yes, they're in a strong room stacked away."

"You'll need to get them out."

Wilson nodded.

"Can you arrange that now?"

"I'll arrange it," said Wilson, truculently and turned away from them to make a call.

"They're going to get them out for you," he said after he finished the call.

"Thanks, see you at the office, Wes," said Clement.

Clement and Rebecca walked in silence to a nearby coffee shop, found a table, sat down, and ordered coffees.

"There is no way I can see of helping Michael with Jack and Wilson working together," said Rebecca after they had ordered.

"Michael is certainly in a very difficult position, I almost wish I hadn't offered to help him."

"It's difficult," said Rebecca.

"Michael Anders needs to be put in control by what we do, but it's hard to see how. We need to talk to Michael," said Clement.

Rebecca agreed, and sent a message asking the heir to GVN if he would meet them for dinner.

Michael replied that he would and suggested a restaurant near where he lived.

24

Andries, the owner of the game farm, was worried about his substantial holdings in both Ngami and GVN, but had not managed to speak to his son when he got Ben's message; asking how he was going in arranging see his son's friend.

He was driven by interest, in his investments, as much as Ben's need to produce the information and replied to say would call Ben back.

Ben looked at the reply and told Paul they would need to wait for a few minutes longer.

Paul nodded wearily and sat back down into the plush foyer chair.

Andries managed to contact his son and explained what the Ngami partners needed.

He was told that the approach being used in GVN's platinum mines in Rustenburg was questionable, with the added commentary, "I've been worried about the directions GVN has been heading down in the past few years. Did you tell the American about Henk, my schoolmate?"

"What should I have told him?"

"That he was the engineer who worked on the advanced mechanized mining equipment study, until a few months ago. His knowledge is up to date."

"So you think the American should see him?"

"If you want him to hear the current story."

"Where is Henk now?

"He's a science master at Bergsig Akademie in Rustenburg. Phone him and tell him what the American is investigating."

Andries called the school friend.

"That's good that you phoned me, Uncle Andries," said Henk. "I could certainly explain the latest mechanized mining trial."

"They've seen someone called Laurens Bredenkamp today."

"Laurens is working in another field of mining now," replied Henk, "His story about low profile mining equipment would be very negative. There is a better picture. Is the American still in town? I definitely know more about the real potential of mechanization of low-seam mining than Laurens does."

Andries sent an SMS message explaining the situation to Ben.

Ben looked at it and sighed with relief, turning to Paul, he said, "Andries has found the engineer who has worked on the latest investigations, into the use of low seam mining machinery, and he says there is a much better picture, than we've been given so far."

Paul was tired and did not want to waste any more time on what he was certain was a lost cause. But still impressed by Ben de Bruin he agreed to hear the story.

Ben phoned Andries and arranged a meeting at the game farm.

The group then left the luxurious hotel to return to the tired looking streets of the once beautiful Rustenburg.

They were followed.

Paul noticed the vehicle behind them as they were passing Protea Park, a suburb of Rustenburg and commented on it to Ben. Ben asked him to call Andries and tell him they were being tailed and needed to change their plans.

"Give me a few moments, Paul. I'll work something out," the farmer replied.

Paul's cell phone rang minutes later, as they crossed the highest point of the Magalies Mountains, at high speed, on the road to Zeerust.

Andries told him to try to outrun the tail, taking the same road to the game farm that they had used before.

He passed the message to Ben.

"What about the gates?" asked Ben.

Paul asked the farmer, and was told that the gates, which were normally shut, would be open.

"If you're happy with them getting that close. They're not far behind me and gaining on us," Paul replied.

"I run a legitimate game farm, Paul. Both trespass and poaching are serious crimes here. We have hunting licenses, and, in addition, there are some protected species of game on our farm."

Ben drove on toward the lodge.

They approached the hairpin turnoff with the four-wheel drive's performance being tested to it's full capability. "Make sure your seat belts are tight," he said to Anne and Paul.

He slowed to take the bend and the tailing vehicle came within range.

Bullets smashed through the back window as Ben slowed to turn off the sealed road.

Anne was cringing into as small a space as she could, as was Paul.

Ben headed along the sand road accelerating fast, now heading in the opposite direction to the following vehicle, which slowed to take the hairpin bend. The gunmen fired again but they did not manage to hit the hired four wheel drive again.

Barely in control, Ben drove through Andries' land and stopped at the lodge.

They got out of the vehicle and looked back at the following plume of dust.

Several sets of double sharp cracks rang out; and the plume slowed, and stopped.

Andries came out of the office and said, "Pleased to see you back."

"Well, I'm not sure we brought you the best of gifts," said Paul.

"We were ready for them. My men were told to stop the following vehicle if they showed any sign of endangering you. They have done so with the skill of people who use rifles in their day-to-day work.

Andries asked them to drive back into Rustenburg, to the Bergsig school, where he said that he had arranged that Henk Wynard, his son's friend, would now meet them, and concluded with, "Do you know where it is?"

"Yes. I lived facing onto the back of Bergsig when I was last here," answered Paul.

"These people must be very well organized."

"And the people you've dealt with?" Ben asked.

"The police will be here to look after things."

"Are you sure?"

"Oh yes, it'll be fine. I've had a lot of trouble with poachers lately. We get on quite well with the local boys."

"Our vehicle looks like it's been through a war zone."

"Take my bakkie, Ben. It's past its use by date, but you won't be noticed in it. You can leave it wherever you find convenient. I'll get the damaged vehicle back to the hire company."

The group then headed back to Rustenburg.

They drove past the vehicle that had followed them, on their way out. It was standing forlornly on the side of the road, about halfway to the farm gate, guarded by uniformed men who, they supposed, were farm rangers.

Paul shook his head and took a deep breath. His professional training and military discipline were telling him to look past the personal aspects of the incident but he was thoroughly annoyed. He said, half to himself, but loudly enough for them both to hear, "This is ridiculous. I'm supposed to analyze a situation impartially while being shot at by the bloody people who will gain from my unbiased opinion."

Anne said, "And they shouldn't be allowed to get away with the rest of what they are doing."

"It's not a moral point, for me. I'm working for financiers, but I sure am finding it hard to concentrate on economics and the practicalities of mining the way you are planning to mine."

25

Ben pulled back onto the sealed road still feeling amazed at the efficiency of his host of the previous day. The dispatch of the threat had been masterly. Andries's quiet, gentlemanly manner and saying of prayers before meals, had given them the wrong impression of his capabilities.

"Let's hope that's the last set of murderous bastards they've got on tap," said Paul.

"I'm afraid it might not be," said Ben.

"It's as though we're in a war zone."

"Like Afghanistan?"

"I'm not sure, buddy. We had guns and body armor. We were equipped for action. In some ways this is worse."

"I'm sorry to have put you in such danger."

"I'm truly amazed at these corporate crooks you're dealing with. They seem almost mindless."

"Terrible, isn't it?"

"That's one way of putting it. I've really had enough."

Anne was silent. She was thinking about how she would explain her experience to her children, especially the sheer excitement of the chase across the Magalies Mountains.

Some thirty minutes after leaving the game farm, they turned off the N4, drove through tree lined streets before turning into the impressive driveway of the Bergsig Academy.

Ben parked in a visitor's spot and they walked the short distance into the building through its imposing entrance.

Paul thought that the Rustenburg academy, its facade, and its grounds, compared well with exclusive schools he had seen in the United States.

They introduced themselves at reception, and explained that they were there to see Henk Wynard.

They were asked to take a seat.

A slim man with slightly graying hair emerged after a few minutes. He greeted them and said briskly, "I'm Henk."

They introduced themselves, and he answered each of them with a formal, "Pleased to meet you."

With the introductions over, he asked, "Could you come with me please?" and led them through side doors and down a passage way, to his office, saying, as he went, "You are in the sights of someone extremely dangerous, as Andries says, and we need to move before they do."

They agreed.

"If you'll wait in my office, I'll get your luggage."

Van Zyl heard about the fate of his two operatives, after the police reported back on their findings about the shooting on the game farm. He then issued an upgraded warning to look out for the group in which the American was traveling with a description of the old vehicle that Andries had lent them.

The security section of the school, although not officially affiliated with van Zyl's web, had its leaks, and the group were located shortly after they arrived there. An attack in the academy was not considered possible, or sensible, so a watch was set up outside the school.

He reluctantly informed Jack Anders of the failure and was asked how he intended stopping Matthew Clement and Rebecca Rosslynn.

"You said you wanted them taken out in road violence that's so common in Johannesburg; but they haven't been in the open since we've been watching them."

At the Bergsig Academy, Henk needed two trips to collect the group's luggage, and then, without bothering to sit down said, "We need to leave."

They stood and he lead them out of the building, through a rear entrance to an ordinary-looking old four-wheel drive.

"Where are we going?" Paul asked.

"The airport. I'm taking you to Johannesburg. I'll explain the machinery trials on the way."

Henk suggested that the three crouch down in the load area so they could get past the watchmen at the gates.

They agreed and he folded the seats to allow them to do this.

He covered them with a rug and then drove the dirty vehicle out through the main gates.

Their departure, from the academy, was noticed.

Henk took them to the Rustenburg airport, a short distance from the academy.

He parked for a few moments, next to a twin-engine Piper and they climbed out awkwardly after he had given them the keys to the aircraft.

He continued on, to the office, to complete the paperwork for the flight and Paul unlocked the Piper so they could wait for Henk, out of sight.

After Henk got back from parking the vehicle, they strapped themselves into their seats.

He started the aircraft, got clearance to taxi, and they were soon in the air, cruising toward Johannesburg.

"Paul," Henk said to the American, who was sitting next to him, "if I may call you Paul?"

"Of course," answered the American.

"We haven't much time, so I'll explain what I think you should know. I've brought you copies of an article on what we have done with mechanized low seam mining," he said and handed a folder, containing the photocopies, to Paul, before continuing, "You guys will have heard the story about the original attempt to mechanize mining that began in 2001, based on a perceived need for a safer, more cost-effective mining approach?"

"That's right, and a great deal of work was done with a bad ending. The efforts were put on hold," said Paul.

"There is a better story."

"And it is?"

"The original drilling equipment and the introduced bulldozer were effective, but the loader was not. The overall effort was continuously hampered by a shortage of skilled labor. The relatively short faces were problematic. Yet by 2004, the determination of the mining company put them on track to achieve fifty percent of reef production using mechanized mining. The mining system was improved, but by 2008 it was clear that the extra low profile equipment was uneconomical and was causing a high dilution of the ore with waste rock. The economic downturn forced a reevaluation, and it was decided to use mechanized breast mining in only one area. The idea being to evaluate and deal with several intrinsic and clearly soluble difficulties before the method was rolled out to the rest of the company."

"And you worked on that exercise."

"Until a few months ago, when I was offered the position of science coordinator at Bergsig."

"The pay from your position at the mining company, would surely have been a great deal better?"

"I've made several careful investments and I had not planned to spend the rest of my life in the mines."

"So, what can you tell us about the single trial?" asked Paul.

"A mining system, with a vertical shaft and associated incline, was selected, where the reef had a consistent dip, and a channel width of four foot two inches."

"Still sounds terrible, but it's nearly twice two-foot-seven."

"The methodology and organization are similar, though."

"Some questions there, I think."

"What reef width do you have in Ngami, Anne?" Henk asked.

"We need Jeffery to answer that question accurately. He makes the operations decisions." Ben answered, and added that he had already contacted Jeffery, to ask him to meet them in Johannesburg, so that he could talk to Paul and Henk, before the flight to Canada.

"Okay. Perhaps we should wait to review the rest of exercise with him."

Paul agreed,

Henk had them in Johannesburg within thirty minutes.

They made their way to a meeting room at the airport, where they found the Ngami mining engineer, Jeffery Nyasa, waiting for them.

Jeffery was given a copy of the report.

"So Paul, what else do you need to know?" asked Ben.

"The main question, I guess, is why what they set up as a second attempt at mechanization was successful."

"I'll tell you about the general situation," said Henk.

"That would be okay," answered Paul.

"A not so obvious, but critical, problem in Rustenburg was that at the start of the change of the operations of the company to mechanized mining, the miners themselves, the support staff and the management were not sufficiently familiar with the approach. Then the implementation was forced through with faulty machinery and the confusion became endemic.

The new and improved mechanized mining model that I worked on was carefully planned using what was agreed as minimum basic backup and support requirements for success."

"So the work was better organized and managed once you started the new section?"

"Yes, we had built a better approach."

"And you reached a conclusion?" Paul asked.

"It worked much better, but I'll come to that if you can be patient."

"Sorry. I'm tired. I've been shot at and heard more explanations than I expected in my most extreme imaginings. So how did you improve the approach?"

"The first change was that development was done ahead of the main ore extraction effort or stoping. At the bottom of each section, a conveyor is installed. A larger loader, than those originally developed was used for cleaning the development ends, and for loading the ore that the dozer pushed into the gullies," said Henk.

"How does that compare with what you're doing Jeffery?" asked Paul.

"We're not working in the same way, more like what Laurens explained this morning," said Anne.

"The development ahead of the main ore extraction, which we are doing, has more head room, which is used by the loader to lift and carry ore to tipping points on the conveyor."

"This bigger loader, was a significant change?" asked Paul.

"It makes all the difference," said Henk.

"Someone like you needs to look at our operation in detail. We've been told that our loader and approach to its use is the latest design," answered Jeffery.

"You mentioned people problems. How were they dealt with?" asked Paul.

"In the original exercise people and particular supervisors had no experience in the use of the low profile, mechanized mining equipment. It was a completely new approach. The management, maintenance and support systems were not up to the complexity of the task."

"We're well set up in those respects," commented Anne.

"Yes, I noticed that," said Paul.

"A training module has been developed, operator training has been emphasized to a greater degree than before. Simulators are used for the practical training of the operators. The technicians looking after the equipment, the supervisors, and the tradespeople also received specialized training," continued Henk.

"We're also right up with you there," said Jeffery.

"That's two important wins but your loader is still questionable. Does the article detail production abilities?" asked Paul.

"They produce about seventy-eight thousand reef tons per month, and they're planning to increase this to ninety thousand reef tons."

"So what's that mean for us Jeffery?" Ben asked.

Jeffery explained that the stope height required by the advanced method was possible in the more horizontal parts of the Ngami reef but said that they were not using the machinery in the way that Henk had explained. "There's something about the loader design that's been used there that's not clear."

"Could you get to Ngami Henk?" asked Paul.

"I can go now if you need me to."

"What do you want him to do?" asked Ben.

"If Henk can see how you can get the loading part of your work sorted out, to achieve the results he describes, then, I think that the risk, of a default on the loan, begins to drop to an acceptable factor."

"That would be great," said Ben.

Paul glanced over the report again and said, "I also think you need to come with me to meet with the financiers."

"Go to Canada now?"

"I don't believe it's my place to establish a case for working the operation ethically, and your sister is an accountant. They need to get a technical perspective of the country, the ecology and the environment and of the geological advantages and their value."

"I'm not sure I can afford to get away."

"You'll be back in a few days."

"Will you manage, Jeffery?"

"Sure Ben, some problems maybe, but we should be okay."

"Right."

"The meeting concluded and they headed off in their different directions

Paul and Ben started off on their 24 hour flight to Vancouver.

They arrived after continuous night time flying, which had allowed them to catch up on their sleep.

26

Rebecca and Matthew Clement found, on their return to the Binnett office, to lay out a strategy for the audit with Wilson, that he had completely lost interest in them and was barely cooperative.

Rebecca could see no way forward, she had decided that there was no way that Jack Anders could be prevented from achieving his goals, with Ngami, and with GVN. That the de Bruins and Michael Anders were on their way to the scrap heap.

Wilson did not ask them to sit down when they got to his office, and greeted Matthew abruptly, ignoring Rebecca.

Clement caught his breath looked at Rebecca, rolled his eyes and said, "Mind if we join you for a few moments?"

"I don't have much time, I've got all my normal work and this extra you are loading us with," said Wilson as he walked, away from them, toward the office window.

Clement sat down and pointed Rebecca to one of the other chairs.

Wilson showing his displeasure walked across, slumped into the third chair, and asked. "What is it that you want Matthew.

Clement said, "Nothing too dramatic, but we must have full access to the South African firm's work records."

"Jack has not agreed to that," answered Wilson.

"Jack is the managing director of GVN. You are responsible for Binnett, so, agreed or not, I am going to prepare an assessment of how much the firm will lose if we stand up to Jack Anders."

"He's actually a valued client, Matthew."

"That's your opinion, Wes, and I don't agree with it, but he certainly seems to have us over a barrel."

Wilson looked away and out of the window, clearly trying to contain his displeasure.

He sighed, realizing he had to provide the basic compliance that Clement was so firmly requesting, stood and went to his desk. He picked up the phone, dialed and asked the person on the other end of the line to arrange for Rebecca to be given access to the confidential files she wanted to see.

After they had left Wilson, Rebecca and Clement worked steadily through until evening; returning to their hotels late that night, after driving from the firm's car park to that of the hotel, thereby avoiding van Zyl's killer who was in front of the building in a heavy pickup truck.

When the pair were reported to be back at the hotel van Zyl included a lookout in the setup at the hotel to signal the pickup truck when the pair left the garage.

By chance, the next morning Wilson decided to show some good will, and collected them in the hotel's foyer, thereby, unknowingly, saved their lives.

The audit continued until the late evening.

By which time Clement and Rebecca had a reasonable picture of the contracts being handled by Binnett, and an up to date perspective of the work the firm had done in Ngami.

They had exchanged ideas of how to use any information they found while they worked.

"Pity we can't extend this knowledge to a site visit to Ngami," said Rebecca.

"That's not possible as things stand," replied Clement.

***

Ben and Paul, having slept on much of the long flight to Vancouver met Ed Chalmers and Clare de Bruin in the financier's Vancouver office building, set amongst some of the, almost crystalline seeming, architecture of central Vancouver.

They were soon joined by the financiers and Paul introduced Ben and Clare.

The group made their way up to the twenty fourth floor, to a conference facility with a view over the bay to the mountains.

Ben stood at the window, looking out on the mountains and said, "This is certainly a beautiful place."

"Isn't it?"

"Hard to picture anywhere with a better view," said Paul.

"We are fortunate. So what do you have for us Mister Cartwright?"

"I'll show you," Paul answered as they took their seats.

He explained the extent of the original project, showing a series of photographs of the smelter, the concentrator, and the original mine.

"Looks substantial," said the softly spoken Canadian woman. "And this part of the exercise is now fully functional?"

"The operation I've shown you took a long time to commission because there were faults in the furnace controls. These are now okay and it's operating to specifications."

"So the problems in the original plant are fully addressed?"

"That's right."

"And the original mine?"

"They've averted a major disaster, and ore from the original project, which was being acquired at great danger to the miners, is now being displaced by the ore from the better designed new operation. The one that requires refinancing."

Paul showed them photographs of the access shafts to the new project's workings, and the beginnings of a future vertical shaft saying, "This is where the refinancing is required."

"The mine does not look as though it's fully established yet," said the elder of the two, a gray-haired man of about fifty-five.

"They are producing ore, as a part of the development."

"How far are they away from full production?"

"Full production is not the issue, it's specific targets that matter."

Paul looked up, into the eyes of Clare de Bruin, and hesitated, before saying, "A key point is that production is being achieved using low seam mechanized mining, which is only effective in one other place."

"Only one? Does that confirm Ngami's ability to hold to production targets?"

"Mechanization needs a more intense management and maintenance regime than conventional mining. Ngami have established the necessary management approach. Their workshops and support for the machinery are sufficiently advanced to achieve what's required. The loaders and the stope design are the points that are not yet clear. The latest information only unfolded on the last day I was there and is being checked by a person who is a mechanized mining specialist. If we're satisfied that Ngami has the flexibility to adjust the loading approach, it's a good prospect," Paul replied. He then half turned to Ben and said, "Perhaps you should explain, the environmental considerations."

Ben nodded and said, "Mechanized mining, like we're using, saves lives and is generally far safer than the commonly used ways of extracting ore from low seams."

"That should mean that it will be generally adopted," said the older financier, "however I've heard that extensive mechanization has been dropped to go back to the old way of mining narrow reefs. Why go back if what you say is true?"

"The main company concerned never completely dropped the measure. They ran into too many problems and stopped using it in the format that it had been commissioned, in nearly half of their operations, to set up one very careful planned and engineered section, where it is now working well."

"So is the method likely to be readopted?"

"That issue is contentious. Poor conditions are something the industry wants, in theory, to move away from. However, in the Rustenburg area, it's not only cheaper to use the many unemployed people, at low rates of pay, in the old ways of mining, but such work also provides a much needed livelihood to many of them," said Ben.

"Labor is cheap in most parts of Africa, isn't it?"

"The northern parts of South Africa are a special case," said Ben. "The area is overflowing with desperate people, it's flooded with refugees. Rustenburg, where the method is used, has the fastest rate of population growth in the country, and the national rate is dramatic anyhow."

"Is Rustenburg where the police shot the striking miners?"

"Yes, and that reflects the desperation in the mines as much as the political situation."

"I see, but can costs be put to these aspects?"

"I believe they can, but not easily in South Africa. In our case though, there is a different environment," Ben answered.

"I'm not clear about why you use the method if it's not economical in the place it was first adopted."

"There's a huge difference between Botswana, where Ngami is located, and Rustenburg. Botswana is the most advanced country in Africa. The measure is more cost effective in Botswana because there are no desperate people, who have to work for very small wages."

"I knew Botswana was famous for its wildlife and unspoiled wilderness, but is cost of labour there so much different?"

"Yes, Botswana a well-managed and adequately populated country that looks after its people."

"That's a poor commentary on South Africa."

"Perhaps, but the backgrounds, the environments, and the problems are completely different. Social progress in Africa is a complex subject," Ben said.

"In the world I guess, so Mr Cartwright, there is an argument for using the approach?"

"Yes, what Ben is saying is correct. I need some additional information from an engineer who I've sent there, but it looks good. On the subject of economics, Botswana could perhaps provide clues as to how economies can be run into the future. It's a very impressive place."

"We've also heard that you are having difficulties with GVN, Mr de Bruin. We were expecting to hear from the heir to GVN who was linked in to our last meeting."

"We haven't arranged for that today," said Clare, the moment of hope dropping away exponentially.

"We need to hear his opinion."

Ben agreed.

The meeting was then adjourned and they arranged to meet again after Michael had been contacted about a suitable time.

***

On their way to the elevator, Clare and Ben thanked Paul for his stronger than expected commitment.

"I wonder how in hell they got hold of the story about problems with GVN?" asked Paul, "I knew Michael was under pressure but those two seemed to be implying something more."

"It will be Jack's doing. We surely didn't need Michael's situation to be brought into the equation," said Ben.

"How bad is it?"

Ben then fully explained how Jack Anders was trying to take control of GVN.

Paul shook his head and sighed, "This has certainly developed into more than I could have dreamed. This Jack guy seems to be half mad," he said, and suggested they talk about what had to be done over coffee when they got back to the hotel.

When they were in the coffee lounge, Paul said, "This corporate performance problem is new to me."

"Binnett are helping sort some of that out, we'll have to rely on Rebecca and Clement, I don't know how they are doing. So where do we go from here?" said Ben. "You seemed to be saying to the financiers that Henk could provide the certification?"

"As a company, but we must get a person, qualified to do that, there, to back him up."

"Rebecca can do that but they've refused to allow her to do anything for us."

"I don't know how we can deal with that," said Clare "We're right back where we started."

"There's something else worrying me," said Paul, "you have one section working, using two loaders, one still in the workshop, and more on the way?"

"That's right," answered Ben.

"The machinery company advised you to use the loaders?"

"They did."

"And you were told they had been designed for your operation?"

"That's right."

"We need to check that."

"Henk could look into the manufacturing background, couldn't he?"

"Yes but he needs technical support on the mine's capability. If Rebecca could do a small amount of freelancing through Henk, she would be consulting for my company," said Paul, "and we are working for new development. GVN have nothing to do with that."

"Okay Paul."

"So I urgently need an order from the Ngami partners, for Henk to do the checks on the extent of the resource, that we need for the bankers; as an extension of the order you originally placed for him to look at themining method."

"What should the order for Henk say?"

Paul explained what he needed, and Clare emailed instructions for this to Ngami.

"Now we have to phone Rebecca and see if she can get to Ngami," said Paul.

27

Clare's call to Rebecca interrupted the late evening efforts; of the sorely stretched Binnett associate, and the firm's principal, Matthew Clement, as they burrowed ever deeper into their firm's links with the more shady aspects of their firm's dealings with GVN.

When Rebecca answered, Clare told her they had to have the certification she could provide and explained how.

"Same problems Clare, we're up to our necks with GVN, Matthew Clement and I are just beginning to appreciate the extent of exposure we have to them, we're auditing their records at this very moment."

"Not good?"

"Really not good."

"Let me explain where we stand anyhow, Paul's with me, and my phone's set to conference mode."

"How did Paul do in South Africa? Does he support the methods you use in Ngami?" Rebecca asked.

"He found that the loading machinery is not right. There are, however, other possibilities and they're being checked now."

"So is the financing approved?"

"No a mining plan has to be agreed, and the reserves and market for the ore must be certified. They have also told us that they need some confirmation of the stability of Michael in relation to both GVN and Ngami. Somehow they've found out about the GVN problems as well."

"That's certainly Jack and the resource assurance is the same stumbling block as before," Rebecca answered as she switched her phone to conference mode and signaled Matthew Clement.

"As I said, Paul has suggested a loophole might exist, if you did the work for his company. He has someone from South Africa in Ngami now, working for him, checking on the mine design, and the machinery being used there, you could subcontract to him."

"Well, I haven't been able to get them to allow me to do anything to help, but I suppose that might be a way, hang on, I'll see what Matthew thinks."

She repeated what Clare had said in case Clement had missed any of the information.

He put the paper he was holding down, stared into the distance for a few minutes, and then said, "I think Paul has given us what we need to take control here too."

"They have explicitly said I could not work on Ngami," said Rebecca.

"Paul's firm is not Ngami. The new project is separate. So, working for him, you would be twice removed from GVN's material interests. You could certify the reserves for Paul, not Ben. Stay away from the older project. When you are there, ask the person, that Paul has sent, to check specific facts, about the old project's progress.

"Yes."

"Using what we have here, we should then have what we would need to help stabilize Michael Anders' position and the de Bruin's would have the assurance the financiers need."

"Right," Rebecca answered as Matthew paused to collect his thoughts.

The principal then continued, "We might then use all the information with the presentation you made in Vancouver to help Michael handle his cousin."

"Okay, so what do you want me to do?"

"Ask Clare to get an order from Paul's firm for Binnett South Africa, for you to certify the new project's reserves, and a separate order for Paul's engineer, to certify the 'market' for the ore. Fax the order for Rebecca to Binnett, South Africa, at this fax number here," he said and walked across to the office fax where he noted the device's number, returned and handed the note to Rebecca.

"Now?" she asked.

"Yes, ask her to let us have an email copy of the order, and tell her we need to get it now, while we're the only ones about."

Although Clare had heard most of this, Rebecca repeated what Clement had said.

The requested digital copy of the order arrived as dawn was approaching, as did the fax.

Clement replied electronically, accepting the order, with a copy to Wilson.

"What are you planning?" asked Rebecca.

"We have an official request from Paul's firm to Binnett, South Africa. I've accepted the work on behalf of Wilson."

"Who's not available?"

"That's right. We don't want to disturb his evening."

"Can you leave for Ngami first thing in the morning?"

"If you say so."

They made a preliminary list of what she had to do, based on the previous year's work, and then made the bookings for her flight.

Rebecca drew up a one-day schedule with a table of statistics that she needed, and confirmed this with Peter Connor, the Ngami chief engineer.

They then emailed this information to Paul and Clare.

Paul replied with a list of additional facts that he needed them to check.

Among Paul's questions was one about the nameplate data from the extra low profile loaders.

Rebecca and Jack Clement decided it was too late to brave the streets of Johannesburg so looked around until the each found a bed in first aid room. There the managed to catch up with a few hours sleep.

Matthew Clement phoned Michael when he woke at eight in the morning and asked to see him.

Michael arrived in about twenty minutes.

Once they were comfortable, Clement gave him a brief outline of what they were planning.

"Sounds like we're getting somewhere" said Michael looking pleased.

Matthew asked him for more information about the board meeting, at which he had temporarily blocked his cousin.

Clement listened and then said, "Was the list of what had happened at Ngami, that you wrote, accepted?" after Michael had explained.

"No," said Michael, and told them his list had simply put his point of view, "It needs some backup, which is one of the reasons I asked for your help."

Clement then gave Michael a more complete picture of what had happened, between Paul, Ben and Clare, in Vancouver and what they had planned for Rebecca's short assignment to Ngami.

"I've been working on the list of the information, I'll show you what I've done," said Michael and produced a tablet computer.

Rebecca glanced over the list, and said that she would be able to confirm each point by using Paul's engineer, with the help of Peter Connor, to carry out the detail checks she would need. "Can you email that to me?" she asked,

Michael agreed.

After finishing light meals, that they had ordered in, they parted.

As Rebecca was looking through what she intended to take with her to Ngami, and preparing the documentation that Clement needed for his meeting with Jack Anders at GVN, she found that Binnett's South African work list seemed to be missing many of the projects that she had recorded the previous evening, using project reports. She decided that Clement would need GVN's own list for the meeting, and rang Jack Anders' personal assistant.

The person concerned knew and liked Rebecca. She told her that the accounts office had recently prepared such a list for Jack but that she needed his permission to pass it on.

"Could you ask him?"

The woman replied that Jack was not contactable because he had gone to Ngami. She said she would check with him when he got back.

Rebecca thanked her and hung up.

Worried that Jack's journey meant he had found out about the work Henk was doing in Ngami and that he was going there to try to block Henk's investigation if he could, using the weight of his position, she phoned Michael Anders and explained what was happening.

"Leave it with me, I'll see what I can do," replied Michael.

She phoned Clement and explained that she could not get him the list he needed and that there was some doubt that Jack would be meeting him, but that Clement was looking for Jack.

"Well, we'll go anyhow and see what happens," replied Clement.

After Rebecca had arranged for the incomplete contracts between GVN and Binnett, that were on her list, to be ready for Clement, to take to the meeting with Jack and Michael, she sent him an email explaining what she had done, and was taken to the airport in a company vehicle.

Wilson took Clement to the meeting that had been arranged with Jack Anders in the GVN building, and, on the way, asked him where Rebecca was.

"She's in Botswana."

"Botswana?"

"That's right. Didn't you get the e-mail?"

"I haven't had time to read my mail yet," said Wilson.

Clement told him what the email was about.

Wilson's face clouded as he listened, "You've accepted an order for her to assess the capability of the new Ngami project?" he asked.

"It's from an outside agency, they were in a hurry, needed it immediately, so I had to make a decision."

"But?"

"Since you weren't there, I decided that she should go. There are a number of things about Ngami that I need to have checked, so the order was fortuitous."

"But Jack..."

"Jack does not control who we take work from."

They arrived at reception as they spoke and the person on duty asked if she could help them.

Clement said he had an appointment with Jack, and they were shown into the conference room where Clement had first met Jack.

When the receptionist returned, she told them that Jack had rescheduled the meeting and had gone to Ngami.

Clement asked her to wait and phoned Michael.

28

Michael had set out to find Jack after hearing from Rebecca.

He was blocked at every turn.

He was still in the safe lay-by twenty minutes later, having pulled his car over, to answer Rebecca's call.

Eventually he checked the airline schedules wondering if he should go to the airport.

The office manager saved him from doing so by phoning to say she had found Jack, and gave him the landline number where Jack could be located.

Michael phoned his cousin and asked, without preamble, whether he was going to the meeting with Clement.

"I don't want to see them just yet," answered Jack. "I'm going out."

"Where are you going? For heaven's sake, man, they're going to an appointment they made with you, and I've been asked to be there."

"I need to go to Ngami. I'm rescheduling the meeting with them. I didn't know about your being there."

"I'd like a few answers myself."

"I wouldn't bother myself, Michael," replied Jack.

There was a moment's silence, then Michael, who had not spoken to Jack since the Monday board meeting, answered, "What about this meeting? They are still expecting you."

Jack hesitated. A scene about something as trivial as a meeting with Binnett would attract too much attention, and his planned surprise visit to Ngami was now no longer a surprise. "Okay," he answered, "let's see what the damn people have to say."

**

When Clement got through to Michael, from the conference room, he asked if Michael knew that his cousin had cancelled their meeting with him.

"I've spoken to him Matthew, the meeting is still on. Both he and I are on our way," Michael replied.

Clement relayed this message to the receptionist, and asked her if she would turn up the lighting and adjust the air-conditioning.

Michael and Jack arrived almost simultaneously.

Jack barely greeted Clement and Rebecca, and then asked, "So what is this schedule you want to discuss, Mr. Clement?"

"There's something else we would like to talk about before we consider schedules," Clement answered.

"I'm not interested."

"Please allow me to explain."

Jack shrugged and nodded.

Clement continued, "We're going to use what happened in Ngami, last year, in a keynote presentation at the mining institute dinner next week."

"Why?"

"Your efforts to shut the process went beyond your agreement with the partners there and with us, and that's what'll be reflected in the presentation we give. We thought it would be better to get your perspective sorted out before the dinner."

"That's a threat, is it?"

"No, it's something we're doing, as a firm, with considerable responsibilities, in sensitive areas, who are in a relationship with your very significant corporation."

"This is ridiculous, Michael," said Jack.

"We should see it, though," Michael replied.

"Mr. Clement, we're a big company and really can't waste time on threats from one of the many consultants we employ," said Jack.

"We're not wasting your time. I think you'll find that what we have to show you will interest you."

Michael said, "I hope so."

"Can I use your system?" Clement continued.

"I suppose we can see what it's about," said Jack and pointed to the projection processor.

Clement started the computer and played the DVD of Rebecca's presentation to the mining and consulting conference in Vancouver.

The setting of the conference came up on the large screen. The backgrounds of some of the more important people at the conference were briefly reviewed, and then Rebecca's presentation was introduced by Clement.

Michael and Jack Anders sat without saying a word.

"Of course you'll both recognize the situation, even though no names were mentioned," Clement said, as the recorded presentation finished, "and now, with what we have found from our local records, together some other details that Rebecca is checking, we have enough information to comfortably fill in the details."

Jack lowered his polished veneer for a second and said, quietly, "I don't agree with what Rebecca said at that Vancouver conference, and don't think she should have said it."

"Is any part incorrect?"

"There's no documentation, if you put our name into that we'll sue you," Jack turned to Michael and said, "We can't sit here and be blackmailed by a consultant Michael."

Although forewarned, Michael had been horrified by the presentation, if for no other reason than that he needed to keep GVN's problems in Botswana out of the press, because of his other plans there.

The consultancy had been clearly shown as being used, by GVN, to defraud investors and the Ngami tribe. If this were to be showed, with identification of the company, at the Institution of Mining's annual dinner, it would be a disaster, frighten many investors, and put Jack out of contention for even a director's position in the company. Michael turned to Jack and said, "Jack you need to take some other point of view here. You can't simply sweep this aside."

"It's all an exaggeration."

"I've just had the information confirmed by Rebecca, who's in Ngami," said Clement.

"In Ngami? What's she doing there? I don't want her there."

"She's working for an outside agency."

Jack glowered at Matthew Clement and said, "What do you want, Mr. Clement?"

"Nothing much more than we originally mentioned. We need to carry out on site reviews of all the work that Binnett are doing for GVN, to gauge the integrity of the work."

"We don't want your interference," said Jack.

"The review will start with a few more points about the Ngami project. The situation shown in that presentation you've just seen, differs markedly from what you said at the board meeting with Michael that was held last Monday. False information which we now believe has been given to the de Bruin's Canadian financiers, even though it is supposed to be confidential."

"That needs to be straightened out now," said Michael.

"We need to do so to make sure there are no other situations where the law, or basic principles and rights are being ignored," continued Clement. "and that with the other details, that we need, will mean this schedule will take several months," said Matthew as he handed Jack a chart.

Without even glancing down, Jack Anders looked from Clement to Wilson and then to Michael and said, "Rebecca's work in Ngami caused us a great deal of trouble, she's not needed on any of our sites. You say she's in Ngami, how can she use anything from there without our involvement?"

Clement told them they had an order, from a completely separate entity, for Rebecca to qualify the productive capacity and potential of the new Ngami project, "And that information relates to the market which you do control which is not confidential in that context."

Clement, watching Jack, thought he had seen a similar expression on the face of a trapped animal.

Jack snapped, "We don't want her there. She's already failed there. What we originally expected was the closure of the Ngami project. We employed your firm to achieve our objectives."

"Our South African office received an order from an outside agency requesting that Rebecca certify the new Ngami project's capability. The new project has nothing to do with you. Are you saying we should stop her?" Clement asked.

"We don't want her there," Jack repeated.

"To an extent, that confirms the implication of the presentation that you've just watched."

"All we needed from you in Ngami was for Rebecca to get to the site and explain that the project was hopeless, and now you are threatening us."

Clement said, "The presentation is a factual account of a nasty situation in which you played a key part."

Jack closed his eyes briefly, hesitated, and then said, looking at Michael, "If they go ahead with that presentation in the mining forum, they'll lower the status and value of GVN."

"It's a factual commentary. Your actions are interfering with our ability to function in South Africa," said Clement, and, thinking of adages about the danger of wounding dangerous animals, knew that he could not stop until Jack was completely out of the picture. So he added, while lifting a bundle of folders from his briefcase, "These are unsigned contracts which you have with us. Could you please approve them."

Michael sat forward and said, "I'd like to countersign those."

Jack didn't reply.

Clement decided it was time to leave. He thanked the two dissimilar GVN directors, looked at Wilson and nodded.

He and the South African principal then left the conference room.

After the departure of Matthew Clement and Wes Wilson, Michael said, "Jack, I keep wondering and asking what's going on, and now these people have put together a case that could destroy us."

"Rosslynn is an opportunist, a clever performer. You need to learn that you should never put your full trust in consultants," Jack said, switching back to his usual condescendingly way, trying to put Michael back into place as his immature younger cousin.

"As Clement asked you, which part of what she showed the conference is not true?" Michael asked, thinking, "Got you at last, you shadowy bastard."

"Clement is simply telling us not to threaten their work with them."

"That's not the only message I'm getting, Jack. What the hell is going on?"

"You can see how they're simply persistent salespeople," Jack said. "We need to show a common front to the shareholders. It will make us look stupid if we allow them to have their way."

Michael hesitated. He knew that what Jack had said about shareholders was true. It was the reason he had allowed his devious cousin to survive the previous year's fiasco, to his regret. He continued, "I need to think about what to do Jack."

"Michael, there's no room for maneuvering."

"Perhaps you should have thought your own actions through a little better?"

"What do you mean?"

"You know quite well, Jack. I need to think about things but for now, I must insist that all instructions to Binnett go through me in future, and I'd like that in writing this morning. We will also need to discuss the reply Rebecca produces about Ngami and most particularly we are going to change the way we're running things at next week's continuation of the board meeting."

"Right, Michael," said Jack softly.

"I'll get that instruction in writing for us to approve, while you go through and sign these outstanding orders for Binnett," said Michael, opening his portable on the conference table.

Jack half stood up.

Michael looked up at him and said, "Please sign them now, Jack. I don't want this to drag out any longer."

Jack paused, looked into the distance, his face clouding, then sat down; stiffly, pulled the bundle of folders that Clement had left toward him, and reluctantly took out his gold-plated pen.

29

On Rebecca's trip to Ngami she had been met at Ngami airport by Peter Connor, with whom she had worked during the complex situation that Ngami had faced the previous year.

They walked in silence to his four wheel drive.

"How are you and family getting on up here Peter?" she asked as he started the vehicle and drove to the survey office.

"Its been a strain, and the continuing uncertainty is depressing."

"Can't be fun."

"It's not, and we've given up a lot to be here. How about you?"

She explained what she and Clement were doing in Johannesburg.

"Sound like a very difficult exercise," Peter said.

"It is, but we're getting somewhere."

They arrived at the offices while they were talking

Rebecca spent her first hour explaining, to Peter and Henk, what information she needed to confirm the productive capacity of the existing project.

The two men then left to collect the information she needed.

She used a further two hours to review the new platinum project's plans, borehole, and survey data.

This effort confirmed that Ngami's reserves were worth several billion dollars.

Peter and Henk checked the statistics relating to the fact that the huge plant was now handling more than its design capability, and Rebecca was able to notify Clement of her success on the subjects of the plant's capacity and the events covered in her Vancouver presentation.

Later in the day the three met up at the new site's workshops, so that Henk could see the loaders that Ngami were using for himself. It took him a few minutes to examine them and he then turned to Peter and Rebecca to say, "They seem to be the same type as those we decommissioned in 2008."

"Surely not?" Peter said and took the information Henk had noted from the nameplates of the Ngami extra low profile loaders. "There isn't anything about date of manufacture here," he said.

"You need to get someone to check the machine numbers and the data there is, with the plant that made them rather than the suppliers," said Henk.

"Let's go to the workshop's office," Peter answered.

They followed him to the office, where he emailed the name plate information to consulting engineers in Johannesburg, asking them to check the manufactured dates for the machinery.

The Johannesburg consultants called back to say that the loaders had been manufactured in 2007 and had been held in factory stock, to be refurbished before being sold to Ngami.

Hardly the recent development that the partners had been told they were.

This was discussed with Paul, who said that since talking to Henk, about the latest developments in Rustenburg, he'd wondered if this might be the case.

Peter Connor then organized a conference call, that included Henk, the suppliers, and Ngami's lawyers.

The suppliers, having stated, in writing, that the loaders were the latest development, tried to explain their false assurances, by saying that what had been said was essentially true, the machines were the latest model, because they had been refurbished with current hydraulics and the configuration of the machinery had been the last modification of the model. Since there had been no more recent development of the particular configuration, what they had supplied was the latest model.

Peter and the lawyers protested at the inadequacy of this, backed up by Henk's exact knowledge of why the mechanical framework, that had been supplied to Ngami, did not perform properly.

In the interest of customer satisfaction, and legal rectitude, the suppliers agreed to take the loaders back and very reluctantly agreed to credit the partners with the full amount they had paid.

Henk, with the Ngami group, sketched out a plan for using more traditional mining in places where the reef was too narrow, together with ways to transition from this to mechanized mining, where appropriate.

Ben, Clare and Paul were then contacted for the concluding meeting, using teleconferencing.

Henk was asked if he could provide guidance with the low profile mining and, after conferring with his employers at Bergsig, was contracted, through Paul to provide ongoing advice for Ngami.

Rebecca returned to Johannesburg the next morning to be met by Michael who had brought Clement with him.

They were completely satisfied with what she had achieved.

The prearranged telephone conference with the Canadian financiers, was held from Michael's home. The more senior of these asked, of Paul, "Does that mean you will now recommend the plans for Ngami?"

"The reef conditions in large parts of Ngami are within the extents that will allow successful narrow seam mechanized mining," answered Paul, "They hae the flexibility to use conventional mining in those areas that are not suited to the approach.

The financier then asked Michael Anders, "Now to the slightly sensitive question of your political situation Mr Anders, for which intrusion I must apologize, but the amount of funding is such that we must be sure of all aspects of Ngami's management,"

"I understand that," said Paul.

"So in regard to the role of GVN, we have had reports about the instability of your position, and even of GVN, in relation to a number of influences including the possibility of Ngami's failure."

Michael gave them a brief summary of what he and his cousin had agreed following their meeting with Binnett, and of subsequent discussions they had held after he was given the copy of Rebecca's report to Paul's company.

Saying Michael had been approved by the GVN board as managing director of the GVN corporation. He also explained that Jack would remain a key member of the board with responsibility for financial investigations and that this would avoid any possible concerns in the stock market about clashes in the corporation's board room.

The financiers nodded their satisfaction and the older said, "That's under control then."

"There will be difficulties, as there always are where ambition and money mix, however, I, Ngami and GVN are in a sound position."

The certification of the ore reserves by Rebecca working for Henk, was confirmed by Paul, who also explained that a solution to the problem of the inadequate loading equipment had been negotiated and how variations were going to be made to the mining approaches.

The new contract for finance of the Ngami extension was then signed.

In it, Paul, Henk, and Binnett were noted as monitoring agents to support the future Ngami development and mining. Paul having agreed to a request that he help the partners in the longer term.

***

On Saturday evening, Rebecca, alone in a hotel in the Drakensberg where she, Michael and Clement had gone for the weekend, tried to read a novel. She could not concentrate. Her spectacular, exciting, and sometimes dangerous, career had again moved forward. Her responsibilities were now well beyond those of an adviser on engineering and organization.

She thought of the work ahead with increasing enthusiasm, and already had plans to contribute strongly to the solutions, that Binnett, in Sandton, needed to implement. She thought delightedly about how she was to become a catalyst in a developing environment, where her decisions would increase the profitability of Binnett. Her expertise was going to become a cornerstone for their growth to a better position in industry.

***

Subsequently Peter Connor and Jeffery Nyasa were given additional responsibilities and took over the management of Ngami from Ben de Bruin, with strong consulting backup from Paul, Henk, and Binnett.

Ben was thus freed to concentrate on another discovery he had made.

***

Paul offered Clare de Bruin a key position with his firm while they were holding a celebratory dinner with Ed Chalmers in the 'Salmon House on the Hill', in Vancouver.

She decided that it would be a good move.

***

Paul had been asked by Michael if his company would be able to help him with the GVN recovery effort he foresaw, and accepted the offer.

***

Ed decided to spend more time in Vancouver, to follow up on his investigations there.

***

Jack Anders and van Zyl had a meeting about their next moves, in Switzerland, where van Zyl was providing security at an international conference.

Neither man intended to allow the series of setbacks, in Johannesburg or Botswana, to interfere with their long term efforts.

***

A week after the agreement had been signed, Peter, Charles and Jeffery sat down to dinner with Peter and Charles's families to celebrate the success of the work done, and their new roles.

Ben de Bruin was guest of honor.

The conversation drifted to Joseph, who had helped find the ore body, and was present.

He was managing well at school, but was having problems with a group of bullies.

Charles shook his head at the news, "I need to see if we can do something about a bursary for Joseph. He has done so well that it is quite natural for people to be jealous, but, of course, there's the chance that it is being done by the same group that have been giving me trouble. I wonder if Jack is still angling out there"

"Don't say that," said Ben.

"No, I suppose the past should be put aside. Anyhow, I went to a very good school in Zimbabwe. Perhaps it would be a good idea if Joseph spent some time there?"

"I don't really want to go away," answered Joseph.

"Perhaps we can take a look together?" said Ben, "I've got to go to Harare myself this week?"

Joseph looked awkward, "It is a bit hard, always dodging them. I've had two fights this week already."

Christine listened to the exchange with a touch of sadness. Joseph had been a pleasant addition to her family.

Dr. Thomas Bagot

ABOUT THE AUTHOR

Thomas Bagot, PhD (MGSM), MEngSc (UNSW), BSc (UNISA), NDT (UNISA), has worked as an operator, a manager, an engineer, and in management and engineering consulting in Southern Africa, Canada, and Australia. He is married with five children and lives in Sydney, Australia.

His interest in writing developed from a wish to develop a field of literature that shows the industrial society and its changes in a real light. One that will lead to better lifestyles for all concerned; together with a lifetime wish to write a book, and, a frustration with finding books he liked himself. A million books out there and nothing to read seemed to indicate a gap.

Other books:

Fiction:
Out of a Southern African Furnace

Nonfiction:
Beyond TQM and TPM: Plant Performance Management
TomBagot@bagotbacl.com